TRACKS TO
HARLON COUNTY

TRACKS TO HARLON COUNTY

TWENTY-ONE TALES OF LIFE AND ADVENTURE

THE PURSUERS

By Charles Paul Reed Jr.

Storybook Adventures LLC

Copyright

ACKNOWLEDGEMENTS

Cover Art by Dona Reed with all rights to Charles Paul Reed Jr. Storybook Adventures LLC
Cover design by Pepper Reed

I very much appreciate the following individuals who read and provided valuable input in every aspect of this work
Gary Buscombe
Mark Church
Martha Weatherl
Millicent Reed Sadler Webb

Also, by Charles Paul Reed Jr.

Trouble in Harlon County – First novel in the Pursuers series

Mission in Harlon County – Second novel in the Pursuers series

Justice in Harlon County – Third Novel in the Pursuers series

The Long Caper, A time travel adventure to 1865 Harlon County.

TRACKS

The true tales of our lives are made
Of decisions reached or pushed away.
Roads we've taken or turned aside,
Memories that haunt but still abide
Though we may lie and truth evade,
Men will know us by the tracks we've made.

© Charles Paul Reed Jr.

This anthology is dedicated to The United Nations Children's Fund and those who search the rubble of man's folly to rescue the innocent.

Contents

Bronco, MARBLES

Ashville, Ohio. Bill Brumley was practicing his marble shooting when the old man approached and looked on for a minute.

"Hold it! You're handling your shooter like a girl." Bill looked up at his grandfather as the old man swiped the back of his hand down the length of his drooping mustache.

"Look!" He plucked the marble from Bill's hand and showed him in slow motion how to hold it between the tips of his thumb and forefinger and then roll it sidewise into the crook of the first joint of his forefinger.

At twelve years old and tall for his age, Bill had curly brown hair that went a bit too long between cuttings. He looked like a younger version of Old Joe, his grandfather's name for himself when he reached fifty. Bill's blue eyes flashed, and he grinned as the old man handed the marble back. Bill set his fist in position with the larger shooter marble clutched between his curved forefinger and thumb.

"Remember, if you're going to do something, do it right!" The older man shook his head rapidly from side to side. "Don't fiddle around with it. It's two moves. First, roll the marble into position and then shoot it. You don't juggle it around. If you practice getting your shooter into the exact same spot every time, the marble will always shoot the same way. If the marble always shoots the same way, you don't even have to look at it. All you have to look at is your target. After a while, you will be a dead shot!" Old Joe held out his hand for the marble and painfully kneeled on arthritic knees to shoot it toward a grouping of slightly smaller marbles in the circle scratched on the ground. It streaked across the surface, barely touching anything before hitting another marble with a clicking sound knocking it out of the ring,

"See?" The drooping gray mustache lifted into a smile. Old Joe awkwardly stood and then moved his hands from his knees to behind his back. He massaged his shooter thumb and then as much of his spine as he could reach. Every part of his body suffered from arthritis so badly that his work was now limited to occasional odd jobs. Shooting marbles was just another simple thing made difficult because of his condition.

Bill had lived with his mother in his grandparent's home as far back as he could remember. First, Bill's mother died of the fever. Then, his grandmother said that her end was near. A few months later, she passed away, leaving Old Joe and Bill to fare for themselves.

Bill nodded. Old Joe didn't feel up to showing him things very often. But, when he did, the boy paid attention. Of course, shooting marbles wasn't just a boy's game. He had seen men in an alley playing marbles many times. But, whereas the schoolboys played to win marbles, the grown men played for money.

Bill practiced rolling the marble into the right position a few times until his grandfather nodded approval. Then he knelt, moved the marble into place, and then let it fly. It hit the target but didn't strike hard enough to knock it out of the ring.

"That's good! The more you do it, the more accurate you'll be and the stronger your thumb will be. You'll be striking marbles out of the ring every time!" Old Joe put his hand on Bill's shoulder. "I need a drink of water. One of these days, when I feel up to it, maybe I'll show you how to throw horseshoes." He turned and headed for the porch.

Bill looked up and wondered where they'd get the shoes. They didn't have a horse. He shrugged. His grandfather was pretty resourceful and would figure that out when it was time.

After the old man went into the house, Bill put his half dozen marbles into his pocket and walked toward Main Street. He had lost quite a few the previous day to some older boys behind the schoolhouse. Ashville was a small town with half a dozen stores, a bank, and a barbershop. Bill never got a haircut at the barbershop. Old Joe would look him over some random morning and say, "You're looking like a girl again. Bring me the scissors." He'd whack at the hair until he had it cut back to the boy's earlobes, then he'd drop the device on the table and say, "Go play."

Bill rounded the corner onto Main Street and approached the General Store. As he neared the doorway, he heard a commotion inside. Two masked men stepped out the front entrance holding handguns and turned abruptly to their left. The larger of the men collided with the boy before either of them had time to dodge. The man's momentum knocked Bill to the ground. The gunmen swore as he stumbled over him. Bill's eyes widened as the man's old holster brushed past him at eye level. It was made of an old brown leather scuffed and scarred. Bill could see where extra bullets slipped into loops at the back of the belt.

The men sorted themselves out, jumped aboard two nondescript horses, and beat it out of town before Mister Henry, the store's owner, reached the door. Bill and Mister Henry stood together and watched the riders disappear.

"Damn it!" I've got to get to the sheriff." He looked at Bill. "Bill, would you stand here for a minute and tell anyone who comes by that I'll be right back? I'll give you a candy."

Bill nodded and took one of the chairs on the porch until Mister Henry returned with one of the sheriff's deputies. "Thank you, Bill. Come on inside." The clerk let Bill pick out his choice of two-for-a-penny candies.

The deputy strolled around the store as if to find evidence. There wasn't anything to see. The men had come in, pulled guns, scared Mister Henry enough to cooperate, taken money from the till, and run out the door in the space of about five minutes.

Bill took his piece of candy back out to the porch and sat down. He didn't get a lot of candy. Money for candy was scarce at home because of his grandfather's arthritis. Bill savored the hard candy and made it last as long as he could. He had scarcely finished it when the sheriff and another deputy rode in with two men in tow. One man had a mustache like his grandfather, and the other needed a shave. Both were in their forties, and both wore gun belts with empty holsters and handcuffs. The sheriff pulled up and dismounted. He went into the store and called out to Mister Henry.

"Bob, you recognize either of these two men?"

Mister Henry looked up and made a face. "Sheriff, the two men wore masks. They were in and out in about two minutes." He stared at the two men. "And they were wearing blue shirts."

"Blue, huh?" The sheriff looked at the two men dressed in worn plaid shirts.

One of the men grinned. "I told you, Sheriff. We were just riding through on our way to Columbus. We ain't robbed no store." He grinned at his companion. "If you'll let us go, I'd like to buy a blue shirt, though. You got any of those?" He raised his eyebrows at Mister Henry.

"Well, yes, we do." Mister Henry shrugged. He seemed baffled that a man would be inquiring about a new shirt while a suspect for a robbery.

Bill saw a smug expression cross the big man's face. He knew then that the man was mocking them. He pointed at the man.

"These are the two men who robbed your store, Mister Henry," Bill said. He moved closer to the Sheriff.

"You're not going to take the word of some snot-nosed kid, are you, Sheriff?" The bigger of the two men looked from Bill to the lawman. "Was he even in the store?"

Mister Henry looked at Bill. "Bill, you weren't in the store. You were outside."

"I recognize his voice," Bill said. "He ran into me and knocked me down and cussed me out. I reckon I can recognize him."

The sheriff squinted at the boy for a minute. He turned to Mister Henry. "Bob, can't you recognize anything about these two?"

"Well, they hardly said anything. I was concentrating on where the guns were pointing." Mister Henry looked at Bill. "Are you sure, son? I don't want to put the wrong people in jail on my say-so unless I'm sure. I don't think you want to either."

"Well, there is one other thing," Bill smiled. "The man who knocked me down has an old brown belt and holster and...."

"Sheriff, that don't mean nothing," the smaller of the two men objected. "There must be hundreds of old brown belts and holsters in these parts!"

"I reckon that's true," the sheriff acknowledged." He made a disgusted face and reached for the key to the men's handcuffs. Bill could see that the sheriff had caught the man's mocking tone as well. "You sure you can't identify these men, Bob?"

Mr. Henry shook his head. "Not for sure."

"Sir. Sir!" Bill waved a hand and took a step toward the sheriff. "Like I was saying, there is one other thing."

The sheriff made a face. "What's that, son? As much as I think these are the men who robbed the store, I can't go with just you thinking you recognize a swearing man's voice."

"Sir, the man who knocked me down had eight loops on the back of his gun belt. Some of them held bullets, and some were empty. If I can tell you which ones have shells and the ones that don't, you'll know I'm right, won't you?"

The sheriff eyed Bill standing on the porch and the men facing toward him. "I reckon that's true. You can't see the back of his gun belt from there."

Bill smiled. "There were two full loops, two empty loops, a full loop, and the rest were empty." Bill pointed at the larger man. "He was one of the robbers. I was only a foot away from him when he ran off."

The sheriff looked toward the man and backed his horse a couple of steps so he could see the back of the man's belt. "Well, I see two full loops and two empty loops. What was the rest of that, Bill?"

"One full loop and the rest empty," Bill repeated.

"Bill, just to be sure, are we talking left to right or right to left," Sheriff Garment stared at the gun belt.

Bill smiled. "Left to right. If you go from right to left, it's three empties, one full, two empties, and two full."

Sheriff Garment grinned. "Damn, I bet you do real good in school!"

"Yes, sir."

"Thank you, Bill. Gentlemen, you are under arrest for robbing Mister Henry's store. You'll be in jail tonight and go before the Justice of the Peace tomorrow. Let's go."

Mister Henry ran his hand from his forehead and rested it on his jaw. "How did you do that?"

"I don't rightly know, sir. I don't forget much of what I see," Bill said.

"Well, thank you for speaking up, Bill. They will probably get my money back. I don't know how to repay you. "

Bill grinned. "You don't?"

Mr. Henry smiled and turned back into his store. He brought out a canister of hard candy. "Reach in and take all you can grab." He laughed as a couple of loose pieces slipped from Bill's hand. "Okay, now the other hand."

"Thank you, sir. I really do like candy, but right now, I'm wondering how many new marbles I can buy with a handful of candy."

THE END

Sarge, SOLD

A dark fear gripped Brownie when old man Ingerstall's elderly field hand, Isiah, said that the Mister had sold him. Those were shocking words for an eight-year-old Georgia black boy in 1841 or any other year. They were numbing words, and silence enveloped both the old negro who uttered the terrible words and the boy. A chain of questions sped through Brownie's mind faster than he could formulate a response.

Why? Brownie's eyes widened for a moment, and he stared up at the wrinkled face in silence. Isiah's hair was starting to go gray, but Brownie, in his blind numbness, didn't really see him. Then, the boy looked away from the big black man and squinted his eyes hard to keep the tears from coming. His mind sped through recent events. He tried to think of a reason for being sent away. He always did his chores. Sometimes he got distracted by a newly discovered hornet's nest, a little romping with the hound, Daisy, or a horse that needed petting or such, but they got done! The Ingerstall farm was all he knew! It was where he was born, and it was where his mother died of the fever. It was where they buried her back over on a little bit of ground to the west of the chicken house. After she passed, he carried the stones that encircled the grave so he would always know its location.

Now the very man, who supposedly named him Brownie, because of his skin color, "dark chocolate, with just a touch of cream," as Isiah quoted the old farmer for so many years, had sold him! He thought that nothing could duplicate the pain of his mother's loss until he heard these terrible words from Isiah's lips. "You have been bought by that Mister Jones what's got the farm over yonder." The big man's arm swept toward the east to indicate the general placement of the property. "The Mister says he ain't got time and energy to keep up with you."

Brownie felt rebellion rise in his belly. What had he ever done to Mister Ingerstall for him to sell him? Sell him! He'd run away! He'd run far away! If he couldn't be here where he knew people, loved people, and they loved him, he'd up and run.

Isiah seemed to read his mind. "Now, you don't go thinking about doing something stupid." He bent down and tried to catch the boy's eye, but the dark brown face turned away from him. Isiah heard a sniff. "And don't go to crying and moping around like a sissy girl neither. That Mister Jones is the right sort of man for a boy like you."

Brownie pulled up his shirttail and wiped his eyes. In an instant, he made up his mind. He looked at the sky and tried to remember if the previous night was full dark or not. He didn't much like the idea of leaving without some moonshine to light his way!

"Anyway, in the morning, you get your stuff together. You do your chores, and I'll take you over in the wagon. You like riding in the wagon," Isiah said.

"I ain't going," Brownie murmured. Finally, he just had to say the words out loud. He knew he shouldn't, and Isiah wasn't going to like it, but the rebellion was heavy in his heart, and they just came.

"Listen, boy, and listen good." The man's hands grabbed the boy's shoulders. "You is sold, and you is going. If I hear anything different from you, I'll lock you in the fruit cellar till it's time to go. The Mister put me in charge of getting you to the Jones' place, and I'm going to do it! Are you hearing me?" The hands clutching Brownie's shoulders were shaking. They were shaking from fear.

Brownie looked up and was surprised to see the panic in the big man's eyes. It was surprising that a man so big and powerful could be fearful of anything. His face was contorted with his warning like it pained him to say the words. But he said them, and Brownie knew that he meant them.

Brownie nodded. He felt the big hands drop from his shoulders.

"Alright, that's better. Now get on and stack those boards over by the barn like I told you yesterday. Do you want to know why you is being sold? I don't know. It could be cause them boards ain't already stacked, or it could be cause you let the dog get in the hen house. I don't know. It don't matter no more. But if it was me, I'd want to do something to make the Mister wonder if maybe he did the wrong thing selling me! Let this be a lesson to you. When the Mister says to do such and such, you do it right away before something takes your mind off it."

Isiah touched Brownie's shoulder again, turned the boy around to face the barn, and gave him a friendly nudge. "Go on. I can't fool with you no more. I got my own chores to do."

Brownie slowly walked away. He was going to need some supplies for his moonlit journey. He'd need matches for a fire. There were matches in a can in the barn. Remembering that gave Brownie his own business to take care of in the barn, he picked up his pace. Matches and a candle would be useful. There was a piece of tarp out there, too. There would be eggs in the chicken house in the morning. He'd keep a couple when he collected them. He'd need water to drink, but he could think of no container of the right size for that. He'd search the outbuildings. Maybe there was something there? The young bluetick hound, Daisy, lifted herself and greeted him when he approached the barn. Once they got inside, Brownie knelt and pulled the dog close.

"I can't take you, Daisy. I is sold, and I can't take you!" Brownie wrapped his arms around the big dog's neck. The tears started up in his eyes again, but he didn't care if the dog knew he was crying. He kept saying that dreaded word out loud. "Sold!" Brownie realized that Daisy was the only creature at the Ingerstall farm with whom he could cry. The big dog moaned in sympathy. That made him even sadder to be going. He was leaving, for sure. He was escaping tonight, or pushed out tomorrow. Tonight, he could decide where he went. Tomorrow there would be no choices. He'd show them! Sold! As he thought of what he would need item by item, Brownie worked his way methodically down his short mental list.

It was well after dark when Brownie stole out of the little storage building that served as his sleeping quarters. He had all of the supplies he'd managed to collect tied up in the tarp with a piece of twine and slung over his shoulder. Isiah and the other black man, Samuel, shared a slightly larger building behind the main house. The two black women who did the housework occupied another. Brownie wasn't concerned about any of the adults, for he knew they were sleeping hard. He was worried about Daisy. If Daisy got startled awake, she'd start to howl, and if she did that, everyone would be awake, and a couple of the men might even come out toting shotguns.

He slipped across the yard to the lane down to the road. Brownie touched the last fencepost and gave it a caress goodbye. The lane would take him north to the main road. Brownie had been to town many times with Isiah to get supplies. He knew the way. The road went half a mile or so north to a junction. His choice there was to go east toward Titustown or west into the wild. He didn't know what was west but was sure capture awaited him if he ventured into town. There was a half-moon, which Brownie told himself was a sight better than either a full one or full dark. Aside from avoiding people, he was also concerned about critters. There were black bears and foxes in the woods. He had spotted bear scat a few times, and he had heard talk that there were wolves in Harlon County. Brownie moved on with his belongings slung over his shoulder, and he kept his eyes open for loose stones of a specific size. If the rocks were too large, he couldn't fling them far enough. Too small, and they would just annoy the wild thing. Wild Thing! That was what he named it, that unknown danger that lurked in the shadows of the giant oaks and the mottled patches of moonlight beneath the pines.

Brownie reached the junction. He was ready to turn west into that dangerous unknown wild when he noticed a light coming through the trees from the house up on the hill. It was a big house sitting far back from the road. Brownie had been unsuccessful in finding a suitable container for water. His sense of urgency and terror dried his throat. Every farm had a watering trough out for the horses to drink. He'd have to zig-zag a little to the east to enter the lane, but it was early yet. He had time. He could slip up the lane and get a drink before he moved on west!

There was a sign at the bottom of the lane, but Brownie couldn't read it. The lane curved a bit around a hill and was a little longer than Brownie realized when he started. He was doubly thirsty by the time he passed a couple of outbuildings. There was light streaming out of one of the two pairs of double windows at the front of the house. Brownie edged forward and was halfway across the yard before remembering that there could be a dog sleeping here. His blood froze at that notion. Daisy was a barker. It was possible that a dog waiting here could be a biter. It could be a barker and a biter! He stood in the shadow of the oaks and listened intently. Was that indistinct sound the murmur of a voice from somewhere? He stole silently toward the house. When he reached the porch, the murmuring was louder. Thirsty! Brownie remembered his mission and circled left around the porch, and came to the horse trough. In the interest of silence, he braced his palms on the top edge and stooped to press his lips gently against the tranquil surface. He puckered and drank carefully to avoid making a slurping sound until his throat and belly were satisfied.

Curious about the murmuring, Brownie wiped his mouth with his sleeve and then climbed to the porch. He tiptoed until he reached the window. With each step, the voice grew louder. He realized then that the big front windows were open to the cool Georgia night.

The sound of a man's deep voice drew him closer. Carefully Brownie edged up and peered in. There were four people in the room. A man sat in a big chair at an oversize desk, his back to the window. A pretty dark-haired woman sat at one end of a sofa with a boy's head in her lap. The boy appeared to be asleep. He had his legs drawn up and his hands tucked under his chin. Brownie thought he was about his own age. An older boy was slumped in a chair, swinging his crossed leg restlessly.

Brownie realized that the man was not talking with anyone but was reading aloud. Brownie turned to press his back against the wall below the window and, drawing his legs up, encircled them with his arms. He listened as the man continued to read.

"Do you know what friendship is?" He asked.

"Yes," replied the gypsy. "It is to be brother and sister, two souls which touch without mingling, two fingers on one hand." The man cleared his throat. Brownie twisted his head around to look.

Brownie heard the woman interrupt. "John, I think that is enough for tonight. It is getting late, and this boy's head is like a sack of flour on my leg," the woman said. Then, she smiled and looked toward the other boy.

"And that one is getting there," the man responded, nodding toward the restless leg. "But let me finish this passage?"

The woman nodded.

"And love?" Pursued Gringoire.

"Oh love!" said she, and her voice trembled, and her eye beamed. "That is to be two and to be but one. A man and a woman mingled into one angel. It is heaven."

"Bedtime," the woman said. Then she laughed. "You are such a romantic!"

"Well, at least Victor Hugo is." The man smiled.

"Brownie turned to peek in again as the man closed the book. Brownie spotted the plain brown book in the man's hands before his eyes swept the room. He had never seen so many books. They filled the floor-to-ceiling bookcases that encircled the room. He knew about reading. Isiah could read a list of supplies. Old Mister Ingerstall read a passage from the Bible every Sunday as everyone gathered on the back porch in good weather. Just snippets. Not enough to get much out of it. But a book like this with a story and such beauty of language was a magical thing. Brownie breathed in the night air and felt the wonder of books envelope him.

The black boy slipped off the porch and retreated down the lane. His heart was throbbing as he hurried back to the junction. There was a final decision to be made there. He stopped and looked up at the moon. He remembered the fear on Isiah's face. He remembered the black man's words about being "in charge." He knew that meant that there would be a price to pay for the old black man if Brownie wasn't there in the morning. A new resolve gathered in his heart. Instead of going west into the wild, as he had planned, he continued down the road to the lane that led back to the Ingerstall farm. He noted the darkness of the house. He slipped into his little shed and lay himself down on some hay.

It seemed to Brownie that he barely closed his eyes, and it was daylight again. He rose and methodically dealt with his chores. His work was half done when the two black men, Isiah and the younger Clem, appeared. Brownie saw a look on Isiah's face and knew that his presence was a relief to him. Then they went to the back porch for breakfast. One black woman brought out the oatmeal and honey, the fried eggs, and a loaf of bread. "You was a egg short this morning," she said, looking sidelong at Brownie. "Is them hens hiding their eggs again?"

Brownie glanced up and saw the sadness in her eyes. He knew she would not dare mention his leaving. Josey was a good woman, a friend to his mother, but it wouldn't do to say something that would make her cry. Black people weren't supposed to cry in front of white people. Black people were supposed to pretend cheerfulness. They could sing of the lonely, the tragic, the pain because the words didn't seem to mean anything then. The white people just heard the melody. Brownie knew that most white people prided themselves on having happy negros. Josey patted Brownie's arm and squeezed his shoulder. The other house slave, Beulah, slipped out briefly when Josey went back inside, ran her hand over his head, and pressed it against her bosom.

All this time, Isiah and Clem sat looking straight ahead. Brownie knew they were saving their goodbyes for later. There were no words of recognition from either old Mister Ingerstall or his thirty-year-old son in the house. The black men finished their meal and then disbursed to finish their morning chores. They were cleaning the stalls and brushing down the horses. Then Isiah hooked up the two gray mares to the wagon. Brownie saw him go to the back door, knock and speak with the Mister on the porch for a few minutes before he stepped away.

Brownie watched. His eyes never left Mister Ingerstall's face. Would the old man come out to say goodbye? Would he smile in Brownie's direction? Brownie watched and waited. Isiah touched the brim of his hat and turned away. For just a second, Brownie thought the old white man's eyes descended on him. He couldn't be sure because the brim of his hat cast a shadow over his face. Brownie started to lift his hand to wave but stopped himself. He was leaving on that old man's whim.

Isiah came back to the wagon and motioned for Brownie to climb in the back. Brownie climbed in, sat on the floor, and leaned his shoulders against the back of Isiah's seat. As the wagon started up, he saw two pairs of eyes looking out the front windows. The big hound loped out to follow like she always did when Brownie was in the wagon, but Isiah warned her off like always.

It wasn't a long ride to the Jones farm. They rode up the lane and stopped on the back end of the big wrap-around porch. A white boy was sitting on the top step. He stared at the wagon and its occupants. Brownie recognized him from the night before and tried to read his face. There was expectancy there. Brownie wondered if the look of anticipation was crowding out a smile or a frown. Was there a friend behind the silent blue eyes or an antagonist? Brownie knew he was sold regardless of the reception he was about to receive. It seemed like an endless nightmare, being sold.

Brownie climbed down from the wagon, grabbed the tarp full of his meager belongings. He heard a grunted goodbye from Isiah and felt the old man's hand briefly caress his shoulder. He waved back without actually looking and walked toward the boy. The future was before him. The brown-haired boy stood as he approached.

"What's your name?" The white boy asked.

"Brownie. What's yours?

"Madison,"

Brownie could feel his legs shaking. He tried to draw some meaning from the boy's name. Was the white boy's name a clue to his true self, as was Brownie's?

"My mother says you are going to live here with us now," Madison said. Brownie nodded. He needed a clue, an inkling of what awaited him. There was a movement in the doorway, and the pretty brown-haired lady he had seen the previous evening opened the screen and stood silent for a moment. She was tall and radiant in the midmorning sun.

"You boys come in. I've made cookies." Mrs. Jones held the screen open so the boys could pass through. For a moment, Brownie was unsure that he was included in the invitation. Had she really said, "boys"? Then Mrs. Jones reached out to touch his shoulder and motioned for him to follow Madison inside. He went into a kitchen sweet-scented from the fresh cookies. Brownie felt relief envelop him as he sat at the table with the white boy. The mother's hand lay gently on both boy's shoulders for a moment. But there was something that no kindness could erase. An indisputable fact hovered in the back of his mind. Despite cookies and milk, and the good intentions that resided in this place, he would always be someone who could be sold.

THE END

Preacher, OF PRIVATE TRUTHS

Twelve-year-old Robert Gracey halted his Pinto pony just short of the railroad tracks. It was a hot August day in 1835. The train's whistle was shrill as it approached the crossing. Robert knew the rules, and he remembered the possible consequences of ignoring that clanging. The morning breeze kicked up leaves and skidded them across the space between himself and the rails. He looked around. The wagons and carts and a few other mounted horses were backing up a few yards away. Robert knew the time to be approximately eleven in the morning, for the new mail train came through Pumpkin, Missouri, every day at the same time. There was nothing to do but wait.

To his right was the little depot. Pumpkin did not have regular passenger service. The train had to be flagged down. To his left, across the roadway, was the feed store. Robert's eyes swept the immediate area. Something directly in front of him caught his attention. At first, he thought it was the wind moving the weeds growing between the tracks, but no, on closer inspection, it appeared to be alive. It was a movement out of sync with the gusting wind.

Robert edged his horse closer. Finally, he made out a terrapin moving toward him in the space between the two parallel rails. Estimating the few moments before the train would arrive, against the speed of the small land turtle, Robert felt a peculiar lifting of the hair on the back of his neck. He glanced to the right toward the approaching engine. Ordinarily, Robert looked forward to waving at the engineer and the porter in the caboose when they roared by. This time, his interest was focused on the critical moments until the terrapin and the ponderous lead wheels of the train might simultaneously cross that short length of the track.

He estimated that the little box on legs and the thousands of pounds of the train would be in that four inches by two inches section of real estate at precisely the same time. He watched with growing alarm as the little fellow seemed to scuttle between the rails as if racing the train. It was halfway across now. Robert hoped that it might decide to take a breather just there. But, no, it moved forward. Skittered, that was the word that raced through Robert's mind. It was not a word that he would usually associate with a terrapin. It usually applied to field mice, roaches, and other small, quick-moving creatures, but just now, it described the terrapin perfectly. The little guy was in a hurry!

Robert wondered if he intended to outrun the train. Did terrapins have a competitive instinct? Squirrels? Yes! How many times had he watched a squirrel dodge right and left as if showing off its agility? Or was it just unable to make up its mind?

Too often, when that happened, there would be a thump. Then Robert could look back out of the wagon and see a small blob of fur in the street, with a twitching tail held aloft that announced the squirrel's miscalculation.

In but seconds, the terrapin and the train seemed destined to intercept one another. The track was vibrating violently. It rose and fell a quarter of an inch on the cross-ties in preparation for receiving the colossal steel wheels. The ground shook. The little animal continued forward, undeterred by the noise, the shuttering earth, or the vibrating steel.

Robert spontaneously cried out then. His voice seemed but a whisper against the background turmoil. "Stop!" He could barely hear it himself. He knew his warning was too late. The engine's cow-catcher crossed the path before him. The engineer waved. The cars sped by. The man in the caboose tipped his hat. The dust rose, and the weeds bent sideways in submission to the greater force of the passing iron and steel, the shrill cry of the whistle, and the blast of hot summer air.

A bit of smokey grit flew into Robert's eye from the smoke-stack when the train passed. He struggled to clear it as he hurriedly approached the track. Both of his eyes teared up, and for a moment, he couldn't see clearly from either eye. Then, he imagined what he couldn't see; a flattened shell spread a foot or two along the track. He imagined the assorted colors of the little guy's innards dripping down the side of the rail.

In those seconds, Robert felt how vulnerable life is. He felt the vacuum in his heart that most people feel when they lose something valuable and memorable. The catch in his throat foreshadowed his sense of being overwhelmed by the inevitable, unfathomable forces that surrounded him.

Robert nudged his horse toward the track. The previously waiting wagons and such rattled past him. The dust and smoke settled, and Robert's eyes cleared as he reached the first rail. His face still held the grimace of pain that came in the last seconds before the big wheels arrived. It was an outward sign reflecting his sense of defeat. Now his eyes swept the rails near, then far, but he didn't see anything. He dismounted to broaden his search.

The little terrapin was not in sight. There was no "grease spot," as his father would have called it. There was no scattered shell, no multicolored innards, no sign of the little fellow at all! Robert rubbed his eyes and glanced about, perhaps to find another person who might have witnessed the racing terrapin hurrying to its demise. Someone to affirm his loss. The wagons and carts passed. There were no pedestrians. Robert remounted reluctantly, prepared to move ahead.

Then he caught the movement barely visible a foot to his left. He could make out a depression between two of the cross ties. There among the weeds and blades of crabgrass; another movement. He leaped from the Pinto again and leaned forward. Only the terrapin's stubby little legs and feet were protruding from the bottom of the overturned shell. They were flailing about to no avail.

Robert realized then that the great draft of air that preceded the ponderous engine had unseated the little fellow and rolled him sideways into the hole. Robert bent and picked up the tiny creature. The head and legs retreated. The box shell settled upside down in the palm of his hand. There was a bit of moisture dripping out. Robert imagined that the terrapin was peeing in its relief, and the boy made a gagging sound. He quickly turned it over and wiped his hand on his pants. Robert mounted the Pinto, cupping the little animal's shell right side up in his free hand. He would take it home, far away from the railroad tracks. Robert would feed it and release it somewhere safe from wagons and trains. As Robert rode away, he had a new sense of what a miracle is. It wasn't a big miracle like they talked about in church. It was a small miracle, and it felt to Robert as though it belonged to him alone.

THE END

Ben Beckett, SHERIFFIN'

A small group of close friends cheered when Deputy Benjamin Beckett stepped up on the platform. He was a handsome man of thirty-six with an imposing mustache. Even a few bystanders applauded a bit, for Ben was well known in Harlon County for his unwavering adherence to the law and his gruff manner with drunks and skunks. He was a man of good habits and a regular at the Methodist Church on Sunday.

Ben, making his first run for political office, was a bit edgy about the prospect of trying to talk people into voting for him. He kept his speech short, pointing out his four years of experience as a deputy to Sheriff Sam Spade, who, unfortunately, had died of a heart attack in his sixty-ninth year.

"I just want you all to know that I'll continue to serve the citizens of the county in the same way that my friend, Sheriff Spade, did for so many years."

Although he'd never admit it, Ben would have preferred that his job as deputy automatically morphed into the senior position upon the death of his predecessor without the need for election-eering.

Then it was Ben's opponent, Bob Houston's turn. He had been late jumping into the race. His speech was much like Ben's. He made much of his brief military experience, pointed out that he had been promoted to corporal while fighting in the Mexican War, and that he had been a resident of Harlon County for most of his life.

"I think we need a hard worker in the sheriff's job, and you boys that went to Texas with me and Captain Ingerstall know that there's no work harder than army work." That brought a titter of laughter. The good old boys that Bob referenced knew that as dangerous as the army could be, about ninety percent of it was sitting on your ass waiting for something to happen.

Unknown to the crowd, Bob had first asked his father, Henry Houston, for a job in the mayor's office when he returned from the war. Before his patriotic adventure in Texas, Bob had labored in the Georgia sun as a construction worker and as a clerk in his father's general store. The first was more work than he liked, and the second carried no clout. He had indeed made corporal and gotten a little taste of authority in the last months before returning home with Captain Ingerstall.

Bob's father had listened to his son's attempt to persuade him to hire him as an aid in the mayor's office and pursed his lips a bit at the suggestion of city employment. Harlon County was not heavily populated. Everyone knew everyone else's business. Two terms as mayor had fine-tuned Henry Houston's political instincts. How would it look to hire his kin? Finally, he decided that it would be better for the good citizens of the county to do the hiring. Nobody could find fault with that. So, he told Bob to run for the vacant sheriff's job. He took one-hundred dollars out of his store's till as a campaign contribution and resolved to keep the Sheriff's election at arm's length after that.

With the gift from his father, Bob set out to organize his campaign. He ran some ads in the local newspaper and had some posters made. The pitch made much of his experience with the Georgia Volunteers and his brief but essential part in winning a grand victory over the Mexicans. But, since Captain Ingerstall had returned with his dead son's remains, Bob had sense enough not to shine his own brass too brightly.

Ben had arrived in the county about ten years later, so Bob could legitimately claim deeper roots. Although Ben's friends told him he was a shoo-in, he was realistic enough to predict a close race, at least, until someone burgled the Bryant Seed and Feed.

The burglary was of goods rather than cash. Deputy Beckett carefully looked over the scene of the crime. A rear window had been left unlocked, and Glen Bryant said four sacks of cotton-seed and some other goods had been taken. It would not have been a big deal had Bob Houston kept out of it. Mister Bryant's store was right next door to his father's hardware store, and Bob knew the owner well. Eager to have an election issue, he built up the loss out of proportion to the value of the goods. Eventually, Bob worked his thinking around to the notion that as the acting sheriff, it was not just Ben's responsibility to catch the thief, but he should accomplish the task by election day.

"You know, Ben has a full month to work with, and if he can't catch the man by election day, he should withdraw from the race," he suggested to the store owner.

Mister Bryant looked at the younger man skeptically for a moment, and then he caught the young man's drift and grinned.

"Well, I think you have a point there, Bob. I'll mention that to folks when they come by."

Ben heard about Bob's contention second hand. He was amazed that the idea caught on so readily. Several people agreed that the challenge seemed a reasonable one. In a bit, Ben came up with a counter-argument.

"Well, you know, I think that dog's tail wags both ways. If Bob can catch the burglar, he should be sheriff, but he should get out of the race if I catch him. After all, the voters should hold us both to the same standard!" Folks nodded their heads at that idea as well. The result was an election that possibly would be decided not at the ballot box but by which man solved the little mystery. The fact that one of the candidates would be acting as a vigilante didn't come up.

The facts of the case were pretty sparse. Glen Bryant thought the robbery had occurred Sunday night. The store was closed on Sundays, but he had been sorting a shipment from the previous day until around six o'clock. To the best of his recollection, Glen had two dozen fifty-pound sacks of cottonseed stacked in a back corner when he left for the day. Monday morning, he noticed that the pile had dwindled enough for him to recount them. Thanks to a hole in one of the sacks, a trail of cottonseed led from the stack to the back window. There was also a small scattering of seed outside in the alley.

Ben studied the scene. Though littered with weeds and boxes, the area behind the store saw a good deal of traffic, so there was no shortage of wheel ruts and horse tracks. It struck Ben that the leaking seed might leave a trail. He searched the length of the alley, but aside from a little scatter just under the window, he didn't see any leading away. That killed his hopes for an immediate *Hansel and Gretel* solution. Both men were left to solve the mystery without much in the way of clues.

Harlon County's families were mainly subsistence farmers, growing their gardens, raising a few beef and milk cows, and a few pigs and chickens. Cotton was a good cash crop in Georgia, but the foothill farms would never grow quantities comparable to the flatlands to the south and east. Ben mounted his horse and rode out to check the countryside for suspicious activity. He couldn't define suspicious but was pretty sure he would know it when he saw it. It certainly wouldn't do to be seen lounging around the jail when a thief was on the loose.

There were two main junctions near town. Main Street dead-ended in a fork to the west, with one going off to the northwest toward Huntsville, Alabama, while a second headed southwest toward Birmingham. Ben rode a short way out each direction, keeping his eyes to the ground, but found nothing. So, after a bit, he went back to town.

The following day, Ben spent some early morning office time sorting through wanted posters. He had not seen any suspicious-looking strangers in town on Monday, but he thought it would be wise to prepare himself by memorizing the faces of any known lawbreakers who might have come to town.

A little after nine, Jeb Wilson, the ladies shop owner, swung the front door open. He was big-eyed with his news. "Deputy, I was robbed last night!" Jeb was a small man attired in a vest, tie, and suspenders. He usually talked with a slow drawl. Today's speech reminded Ben of a string of firecrackers.

Ben slid his leg off the desk and stood up. He dropped the wanted posters and ran his thumb and forefinger down the ends of his drooping mustache. "What did they take, sir?"

"I had half dozen crinoline petticoats hung just forward of the back room. I noticed this morning that they are missing." He paused as if for emphasis. "And the window on the alley is open!"

Ben felt his pulse rise. His voice betrayed his dismay. "Let's go take a look, sir!" He picked up his hat, and they hurried to the door. He was barely able to contain himself long enough to hold the door for the merchant. In five minutes, they had rushed the two blocks to the store. Mrs. Wilson was peering out the window when the two men entered.

"Whatever, are you going to do to stop these thefts, Sheriff?" she said impatiently.

"It's Deputy, ma'am," Ben corrected as he lifted his hat. "The thief came in the back window, Mister Wilson?"

"Yes," Jeb stepped around his wife and led the way. He pointed at the open window and stepped back for Ben to approach.

Ben inspected the area around the window. He lowered it, then raised it. It was snug in the frame. The locking mechanism looked to be in working order. He ran his finger back and forth on the sill but saw nor felt any sign of a tool used on it.

"Locked for sure?" He looked at Jeb. Mrs. Wilson had followed them and stood at her husband's elbow.

"It's always locked except when we're working back here. I assure you that we make sure it's locked." Jeb protested.

They heard the front door close. Both of the Wilson's turned toward the sound, and in a moment, Mrs. Wilson greeted the arrival of Bob Houston. "Mister Houston!"

"How are you today, Ma am? I just heard about your break-in." Bob slipped by the lady and joined Ben and Jeb. "So, our thief is at it again!" He bent to examine the window. He glanced back at the deputy. "Ben, this is beginning to look like a crime wave. I've heard of this sort of thing happening in cities, but Titustown?" Bob ducked his head back inside and faced the three. "I've done some reading recently on this subject in case the citizens decide to elect me," assured the Wilsons.

Ben felt his face grow scarlet. He tugged at his mustache hard enough to wince. Was that an inference that perhaps something was lacking in current law enforcement? He swung around to face Jeb. "So, you are certain you locked the window?"

"Oh, I locked it," Bob interjected. He grinned. His voice was almost gleeful. "I personally checked all of the windows of the shops yesterday evening!"

"Yes, he did," Mrs. Wilson said, nodding. "I thought it very professional of him to do so, too!"

Ben looked from face to face. All eyes had turned toward him. For the first time, he felt a tinge of doubt about his own efforts. He made rounds of the storefronts every evening, looking in windows and checking security, but it never occurred to him to check the back windows of all of the stores. He wanted to point out that Sheriff Slade never checked windows, but that seemed like making excuses. No one had directly accused him of dereliction of duty, but Bob Houston had a smug expression on his face. Ben moved to the back door. "I'm going to check the alley." He stepped out and closed the door behind him before Bob could follow. He needed to study the surrounding area first hand, and he needed time to think!

Located two doors down from Mister Bryant's Feed Store, the two businesses were separated only by Mayor Houston's General Store. If Bob Houston had secured this store's back window, how did someone enter and steal merchandise? It didn't make sense! Ben reflected that Bob was limited to the same paltry clues as he was, but he reminded himself that he was the law officer. If push came to shove, there was a good chance that voters would weigh his failure on a different scale than they would his opponent. He reflected for a moment on the baffling question of where the thief might strike next.

He could do a stakeout or a patrol of the alleys in town that night. But where? There were stores on both sides of Main Street and three short side streets. A clever thief could let him pass and wait for a few minutes before making a quick strike! The odds were terrible.

Then, Ben realized that the nature of the stolen items didn't add up, and someone was seemingly gaining easy access to locked places. Then he remembered that Mister Bryant often took produce and such in trade for merchandise and sometimes displayed them in his store window. Ben puzzled on the mystery as he walked down the alley and entered Mister Bryant's Seed and Feed store to purchase a few items he had noted when making his rounds the previous evening.

"Have any strangers shown up since yesterday?" Ben asked. "I've been keeping an eye out for strangers, and I've gone through all of my wanted posters."

"No, Deputy. Bob Houston was in here for a bit to ask the same question." Glen Bryant scratched his chin. "I have seen a lot of Bob lately. He has stopped in every day this week. Guess he's pretty serious about that sheriff job." He gave Ben a long look.

"That right?" Ben nodded and picked up his purchases. "Well, thank you, Sir. I'll keep working on it."

The following day, Ben arrived early at Mayor Henry Houston's General Store. He waved at Mister Houston, who was atop a short ladder stacking merchandise. Ben set a paper sack down on the counter. Houston finished his work just as his son entered the store with Mrs. Helen Ables' old black slave, Daniel Grimshaw, in tow. The man was sixty-five years old and stiff in the joints. He worked odd jobs around town. The word was that his earnings went to the widow Ables' purse and kept them both out of the poor house.

"So, we have both candidates in my store at a perfect time. Deputy, I was about to fetch you. I'm missing a large burlap sack of coffee beans." Before he could continue, his son interrupted.

"Don't worry, Pa! I have your coffee." He turned to Ben, "and I think I have our burglar, Deputy." Bob stuck out his chest and gave Ben a triumphant grin. "I was searching the sheds behind the stores on the side streets this morning. Behind Mrs. Ables' boarding house, I found this here sack of coffee, Mister Bryan's cottonseed, a sack of oats, and seed corn. And, hidden in a corner were some women's things. I just brought this here sack of coffee beans with me." Bob pushed the old negro toward a chair and set the beans on the counter before he swiped his hand on the back of his pants leg.

"Old Dan?" Ben pursed his lips. He knew from the black man's expression that he would deny everything. But first, Dan pushed his chin out and set his mouth as he gazed with stubborn solemnness straight back at the three men. Then the old man responded.

"Mister Deputy, I ain't got no use for any of them things, and I ain't never stolen nothing I didn't need. Besides, Mrs. Ables and me don't never drink nothing but well water, hot tea, and a little whiskey when we can get it." He looked up at the two white men and then got to his feet. "Mrs. Ables done told me to take the sheets and pillowcases off the clothesline, and I need to get to it."

"Deputy, I caught him red-handed," Bob Houston snarled. "Arrest him, or we'd like to know the reason why not! Right, Pa?" He looked at his father and wiped his hand on his trousers again. Ben felt a chill run through him at the thought of justice being at the mercy of Bob Houston.

"Well, that's wonderful, Son!" The elder Houston looked at his son with a mixture of surprise and satisfaction. He cocked his head and gazed at Ben. The deputy looked from the old black man back to Bob and his father.

"Unless you found the stolen items in Dan's possession, your evidence is what we in the sheriffin' business call circumstantial. Those sheds along the alley are hardly ever locked. Was the shed behind the boarding house locked?"

"Well, no, but who else would put stuff in there?"

Ben smiled. "If we knew that, the evidence wouldn't be circumstantial, would it?" He turned to the old black man. "You go on, Dan. If I need you, I'll know where to find you."

"Yes, sir." Old Dan grinned at the father and son and shook his head. "It is right worrisome you taking me away from my chores, sir."

Ben waved the old man off and turned to gaze toward Bob. Then he picked up the paper sack and walked over and sat in the chair. "I appreciate you for finding these goods. I'm sure that Mister Bryant and Mister Wilson will be right glad to get their things back. I don't think you solved the mystery, but I think I might have. I see you have the sack of coffee beans with you. Would you set it on the floor here by me?"

Bob picked up the large burlap sack and plopped it down on the floor by Ben's chair. Ben gingerly looked it over without touching it. "So, tell me, Bob, how did you happen to be looking in the sheds behind the buildings down that particular street? What about the sheds down the alley out back?" He pointed toward the back of the store.

Bob's eyes widened for an instant. "Well, I searched the buildings out back yesterday evening, but it started getting dark before I could get down the side street." Bob's face twitched a bit. He wiped his right hand on his pants again.

"What time this morning did you start?" Bob's eyes flicked toward the elder Houston and back toward Bob.

"About an hour ago." He glanced at his father, and his eyes fell to the sack on the floor.

"So, you went directly from home. You haven't been in this store since yesterday?"

"No," Bob glanced at his father again and back to Ben.

"Well, Bob, that's interesting."

"Deputy, you seem to be dancing around something," the mayor said. "You let the culprit go, and now you're asking for unimportant details. What does it matter when Bob searched the shed? The only thing that matters is that Bob found the merchandise, including that sack of stolen coffee!" The elder Houston's voice sounded aggravated.

"Well, Sir. I think it does matter. You see, if you look very carefully at this sack of coffee, you will see some green streaks in different spots. If you look at Bob's hands and pants where he keeps rubbing his hands, you'll see some of the same green markings.

"So what?" The elder Houston took a step forward, but there was a hint of indecision. It had dawned on him that there was more to the situation than yet revealed.

"Well, Sir, that's what I'm getting at. Bob wasn't the only candidate for Sheriff out roaming around last night. In fact, I came by here about ten o'clock, myself." Ben opened the paper sack he had brought and took out a jar of honey and a bottle of green dye. "You see, when you mix this green dye with honey, you get a green, gooey, sticky mess. When I bought the honey and dye from Mister Bryant yesterday, he told me that the dye is a permanent kind. So, I spread a little of that sticky stuff on the outside doorknob of this store's back door last night. So today, Bob comes in with green stained hands and more green mess on your sack of coffee beans. I can only see one way that could happen."

Ben held up the honey. "Can you explain that, sir?" He swung the jar of honey toward Bob. "Or you, sir?" His head turned toward the mayor.

The father and son exchanged a glance. Bob didn't seem to know what to do with the offending hands. The father's face looked suddenly troubled.

"Here's what I think happened." Ben leaned back and tugged his mustache. "I think Bob has a key to this store." Ben leaned forward challengingly. "He does have a key, doesn't he?

The mayor nodded.

"I thought so. I believe that Bob, here, took advantage of the proximity of this store to the ones on both sides. I think he slipped in Mister Bryant's store and unlocked the window. I think he told Mrs. Wilson that he was making sure her window was locked when he was really unlocking it.

Mayor Houston looked stricken. He leaned toward his son, teeth flashing.

"Tell me you didn't do this!"

"I didn't do it!" Bob yelled quickly, but he put his green-stained hands behind his back.

"Now, I figure that Bob wanted to get elected Sheriff, but he wasn't sure that his time in Mexico could get him over the hump with the voters. So, he decided to stack the deck." Ben paused and silently put the honey and the dye back in the paper sack and waited. The father and son seemed to recognize the bind they were in at the same time.

"What if I withdraw from the race? I'm already returning everything that I took. Can't we just let bygones be bygones?"

Bob looked toward his white-faced father. "It was more of a prank than anything else. I don't even want to be Sheriff!"

"Mister Mayor, what do you think about that?" Ben sat back and waited. "Like he said, in the end, since he recovered everything, nothing was actually stolen."

The Mayor nodded his head enthusiastically. "That's true." He paused. "That sounds right and solves everything, doesn't it?"

"Well, almost. Bob is returning all of the stolen merchandise." Ben pressed his lips together and seemed to study on it. "There is the matter of the false accusation of old Dan Crenshaw. A man of his station has it hard enough without being labeled a thief."

"I could give him the coffee," the Mayor said eagerly.

"How about a box of tea instead?" Ben inquired. "And an apology from Bob?"

After a moment's hesitation at the prospect of apologizing to a black man, both men nodded their heads in agreement.

"And Bob will put out the word today that he's decided not to seek election and advises everyone to vote for our current deputy?" the Mayor said hopefully.

"Well, that is your idea," Ben said. "I'm just going to report that the stolen items have been recovered. So that being the case, it is all resolved."

THE END

Bronco, BRONCO ENTERS

Bill Brumley's beloved grandpa had gone to his reward when the young man walked away from the little rented house on Greentree Street in Ashville, Ohio. He had most everything he owned tucked into a small carpetbag.

Bill was seventeen on the hot July day when he knocked on old Mister Sam Jacobs' door seeking a job. He could tell that the older man was skeptical. Bill couldn't know that Sam was calculating low odds that Bronco would last the week. Bill was tall and thin. He had brown curly hair, blue eyes, with a bit of peach fuzz barely visible on his upper lip. He had good teeth and a strong jaw. But the horseman was not swayed by the ready smile and the false assuredness. The one thing in Bill's favor was the difficulty of finding help just then. Thousands of Ohio's men and boys were out of the state, answering Mister Lincoln's call to save the Union.

Bill didn't even know that Jacobs raised and traded horses, though, at that moment, there was scarcely a horse on the place.

The buyer came through every three or four months looking for new riding stock. Mister Jacobs and his middle-aged hired hand, Edgar Andrews, were expecting a shipment of wild mustangs from out west in a day or so to be broken and sold to the army.

Bill was relieved when Mister Jacobs hired him. The old man showed him where to stow his things and introduced him to Edgar. Early on, Bill overheard Edgar's judgment on his fitness as a hand as the two older men watched the boy tackle the pitchfork.

"In my opinion, the kid is near worthless," Edgar said in harsh judgment. Edgar kicked the bottom rail of the fence to punctuate his words. He had a straw clenched between his teeth. "Oh, he's likable enough, and he's not a laggard, but he's a lightweight."

Bill's face held a determined frown as he ineptly dealt with one half-full fork of hay after another. What didn't scatter before reaching the loft was just catching the rim. Bronco's face was glistening, and his shirt was wet, sticking to him with sweat.

"See that?" Edgar said. "You and I can pitch twice as much, twice as far. He just doesn't have the heft to get it done." It seemed to Edgar that a smart man like Sam Jacobs ought to see the difference between this kid's work and a grown man's.

"Well, if he can't do the job, he'll know it about as soon as we do," Mister Jacobs said half aloud. "Remember that Johnston boy, Liam? He was big and stout, but he took a break between every toss. And he was bigger than Bill and two years older." He looked at his foreman out of the corner of his eye. Edgar was about the same height as the old man, but he was more muscular and firmer in his upper body. He was back from Tennessee after fighting under General Grant at Vicksburg. His reward for his patriotism was some nasty-looking shrapnel damage to his right leg and a healed-over hole in his side from a mini ball. He managed to survive his doctoring and leg it home afterward. Edgar fervently believed that he saw the Rebel who shot him. The young man was tall and skinny like this kid. He was wearing a gray uniform, and Edgar believed their eyes had met just before the Rebel pulled the trigger. Then the bomb blew up fifty yards away, and Edgar was thrown topsy-turvy. By the time he came to, the young Rebel had disappeared. Had the mini ball been two inches to the right, Edgar would have been gut shot, which would have killed him, he was sure. So, when Edgar saw the newly hired Bill Brumley coming out of Mister Jacob's house, he imagined that he was looking at the same kid. But, of course, he wasn't. Bill told him right off that he grew up down the road a piece and was never out of the state of Ohio. Still, the likeness negatively affected his view of the young man.

Mister Jacobs knew nothing of this imaginary comparison. He just needed help, and a man standing in his doorway looking for a job was worth half a dozen down the road. As he compared Bill's inept efforts with Liam Johnston and his lazy ways, Bill, for all of his physical shortcomings, was eeking out a near tie. Mister Jacobs smiled. It was kind of funny watching the boy fork the hay and swing it skyward. Not knowing how to pack it on, a goodly amount fell off the pitchfork about halfway up and drifted down the young man's collar. Mister Jacobs admired how the boy would swat the hay away and dig in again. Youth! He still remembered how youth felt. Youth held its blessings as well as curses! He cut the conversation with Edgar short.

"Edgar, go spell the boy and give him time to take a break and get a drink. We need to get that hay stored today. The horses are due to arrive tomorrow."

"Yes, sir." Edgar spat the straw out of his mouth and let himself through the gate. He watched Bill heft another forkful. "Bill, get off the wagon and go get a drink. Just watching you tires me more than doing it myself."

Bill looked around and caught the older man's eye. He was grateful for the respite, though he resented the understated criticism. Bill dropped the pitchfork and combed his hands through his hair to brush out the stray hay. He unbuttoned his shirt and shook it out before he jumped lightly out of the wagon. He walked toward the gate, where a bucket and tin dipper waited. "It's hot today, ain't it, Mister Edgar?"

"It is." Edgar sat down on the rear of the wagon and swung his legs around before getting back to his feet. "Now, sit over there in the shade for a bit. Mister Jacobs says those mustangs will be here tomorrow for sure. We need to get this hay up. We'll have our hands full breaking them after that."

Bill stopped dead still at the mention of breaking the wild horses. He was prepared for any kind of regular manual labor, but climbing on a wild horse broke him into a cold sweat. His first instinct was just to keep walking. He fought down the urge and resolved to think the situation over before acting on impulse.

Edgar picked up the pitchfork and stabbed deep in the loose hay, and filled the fork. He brought the full load up with a lunge and threw the bundle skyward to land well inside the loft. Then, he brought the fork back in a gliding motion and lunged with his body for another load. Again, with packed hay on the fork, Edgar pitched it up. He launched another load and another before he deigned to pull out his bandana and wipe the gathering sweat away. Edgar glanced over at Bill, sitting in the shade. He was surprised to find him watching so intently. "What?" He stuffed the rag into his hip pocket.

"Nothing, I was just watching how you make that look so easy," Bill said. "I'm going to try it your way when we switch up."

"Dang, kid," Edgar muttered. He lunged into the hay pile and brought up another big load. He allowed that the kid was eager, but he just wasn't big enough yet!

The grumpy older man and the willing young one switched off on the work for the rest of the afternoon. They'd drive the team out to the hay meadow and fork the hay into the wagon. Then they'd return to the barn to pitch it up into the loft. The boy did better with the loading of the wagon, as the pitch distance was shorter. It was hard work. Edgar could not see how the kid could last the week. It was near dark when they finished up. They went into the house for supper.

"How's it going?" Mister Jacobs looked up from the table. He was working on some accounts. "I got a telegram. Our fifty head of wild mustangs should be here mid-day tomorrow. They're coming all the way from Abilene, Kansas."

"Any idea when the army procurement man will be along?" Edgar picked up a plate and scooped some beans, and broke off a hunk of cornbread.

"Nah. I haven't heard from the trader since March. I'm sure they'll show up soon enough. It's going to take a while to get this wild bunch ready. Nowadays, boys enlisting are leaving their horses at home. So, having enough to go around is pretty much up to the army."

"I'd want to take my own horse if I had one," Bill said.

"Not if you saw what happens to them," Edgar snorted. "I bet you there's two horses kilt for every rider. Them Rebels get a kick out of using horses as target practice."

"Oh!" Bill ladled in some beans and broke off a piece of the cornbread. He compressed his lips and sat down. He was quiet for a moment while he bit into the cornbread. The beans were still steaming. He blew on them and took a bite. "I ain't never had a horse of my own, but if I did, I guess I'd want to spare him, too."

"Well, by tomorrow at this time, you'll have about fifty to break and call your own until the buyer shows up," Mister Jacobs said.

The revelation of the part they expected him to play with the arriving horses gave Bill another chill. He hadn't mentioned that he'd never been on a horse in his life.

"You boys, hurry up. I want to go to bed."

Bill finished his eating. "Sir, what day is it?" he looked at the old man.

"I reckon it's Thursday. Why do you ask?"

"Well, that hay itches like the dickens, and I was hoping it was Saturday so I could wash it off."

"Go jump in that horse-trough, boy!" Edgar groaned. "And hurry up, I'm going to be right behind you!"

"I think you should go first, sir," Bill replied. "My grandpa always said, age before beauty!" He smiled.

Mister Jacobs laughed. "He's got you there, Edgar!"

"Yeah," Edgar got up and rinsed his plate and fork off at the sink. Then, he picked up the soap and headed for the watering trough at the side of the house.

"You ever do much riding, son?" Mister Jacobs regarded the young man who was still forking beans into his mouth.

"No, Sir. We never owned a horse. We had a milk cow, and I'm good at milking."

Mister Jacobs frowned at this information. "Well, these horses coming in will be as wild as they come, I expect. So what we'll do is take a turn at breaking them. Edgar will have at them first. Then, after he's given it a go, I'll climb aboard. That will tire them out some more. Then, hopefully, when it's your turn, they'll be so worn out they'll be bored with the whole thing and quit bucking."

"Bored?" Bronco's hand froze halfway to his mouth. Being responsible for breaking the horses was worrisome. He felt another shiver of dread run through him. He wasn't entirely ignorant about horses. He had been around them some. But, living in town, his grandfather had always said you might as well throw money in the fireplace as feed a horse. There had just never been an occasion for him to ride one.

Mister Jacobs sensed hesitation. "Yeah, bored is what a horse feels after he has bucked out all the vinegar. Of course, some have more vinegar than others." The old man saw the fear pass across the young man's features. Maybe Edgar was right? Did the boy have the fortitude to jump on a huge wild beast?

Edgar stomped into the room wearing a towel around his middle. "Bring the soap in when you're finished." They could see his bare torso along with the ugly scar from the mini ball and on his legs more scars from shrapnel. He looked sheet-white below his red neck and tanned lower arms. He almost glowed in the flickering candlelight.

Bronco jumped up and rinsed his plate. He had his shirt off by the time the door slammed behind him.

Edgar hesitated for a moment before heading for the back room. "You sure you want to put that boy on a wild horse?"

Mister Jacobs grimaced. "Maybe not. I've got a feeling that he is plenty afraid of climbing up on one."

"That ain't a good thing around here," Edgar said.

The horses showed up at ten o'clock the next morning. There were forty-nine mustangs of every description. One of the wranglers told Mister Jacobs that one had died in the stockcar. Bill opened the gate for them and watched their chaotic passage into the pasture. The fear in their eyes only heightened his own. He had heard somewhere that mustangs were small horses, but they didn't look small to him. They shouldered against each other with brawny thuds that he knew could crush a man if he was in the way. He wondered what he had gotten himself into as they whinnied, bared their teeth, and tried to rear.

"We'll give them a chance to settle down overnight and tackle them tomorrow," Mister Jacobs said. Edgar stared straight ahead, stoic. With Bill being so green, the brunt of the breaking would fall on him again. Edgar could see that Bill was as wild-eyed as the horses. It wouldn't surprise him if the boy legged it during the night.

But Bill was still there the following day. After breakfast, Edgar rode out into the pasture and lassoed a small mare. She resisted some, but he eventually led her into the corral. They loved on her for a while, giving her a chance to settle down so she could get used to being touched, learn the smell of men and leather, and hear their voices. Mostly they wanted her still enough to throw on a blanket and saddle. When they did, the mare's eyes went wild again, with primal fear. She bucked the saddle while she ran the corral's perimeter fence. The men stood and watched in silence until Bill spoke up.

"Seems mean, don't it?" He bit his lip as he hadn't meant to say the words out loud.

"It does," Mister Jacobs agreed. "This isn't how I like to break horses, but these are needed right now, and it would take too long to gentle break them. So, we'll have to be mean now and hope someone down the line will be kind. He eyed the mare now standing against the far fence. "I guess you're up, Edgar."

Edgar nodded and walked out with his rope. The mare moved to keep herself as far from him as possible. The near end of the corral narrowed, so as Edgar moved and cut off the horse's retreat around either side of him, it gradually found itself with less space to maneuver. Finally, he lassoed the animal and brought it close. Edgar tossed the end of the rope to Mister Jacobs and gave the saddle cinch a tug to tighten it as snug as possible. He shoved the mare's right hip against the fence and stepped into the stirrup from the left side. In a moment, he was astride. Mister Jacobs simultaneously lifted the loop from the horse's neck, and she was off again. She was small, and Edgar's bulk worked against her. In a bit, she stood rigid on stiff legs. Edgar dismounted and brought her over. Mister Jacobs climbed into the saddle. Her little breather between riders gave the mare a new spurt of energy, and she bucked a few times as Mister Jacobs held on. Then she tired again, her head hanging low. The old man touched her with his bootheels, and she came forward to where Edgar and Bill were waiting.

"Your time, Bill," Mister Jacobs dismounted stiffly. "Push into the stirrups and try to stay balanced. I don't think she'll give you too much trouble."

With quaking legs, Bill swung his leg over and waited. The horse stood stock-still. Growing impatient, Bill kicked the horse's ribs a mite. The animal took a few steps. He kicked again, and the mare followed the corral fence with an occasional prod from Bill. He rode her around several times before he dismounted and looked at the two men sheepishly. "I guess she is bored?" He stroked the horse's neck. He felt better about the prospect of riding now and downright appreciative toward the mare.

"Well, we have forty-eight more horses to make this way," Mister Jacobs said. "Go get us another one, Edgar."

In the space of the next five hours, the men skipped lunch and worked their way through a good number of additional horses. Finally, after coming to a standstill, the horses were unsaddled and turned into a separate pasture from the wild ones.

"I'm getting too old for this," Mister Jacobs said as they unsaddled the fifth horse. "Bill, why don't you take the second spot on the next one. I think you are a natural horseman." The old man grimaced. He realized that his aching joints were coloring his judgment some.

Bill's eyes widened. It was true that the preceding horses had not fought him much, but he was sure that was because they had all the energy drained out of them by the time he climbed aboard. Moreover, he had seen that riding second was a lot different than riding third. "I'm hoping that the next one is easy," he said. He looked at Edgar. The older man was still breathing hard from his exertions.

"You're welcome to take on the first spot if you're feeling feisty," Edgar murmured. He looked at his hands. Edgar had new blisters on his palms even with the gloves, and the backs were beginning to get raw. Nevertheless, he had managed to stay on for the first five horses.

"Just two more?" Mister Jacobs raised his eyebrows. Edgar nodded. He went off to the pasture and brought out a big roan. He was at least fifteen hands tall and resisted the bit more than the previous horses had. They went through the routine of loving on him and letting him get used to their smell, but the glare never left his eyes, and his ears were laid back even before Edgar threw on the blanket and saddle for the preliminary buck-and-run around the corral. Once Edgar was up in the saddle, the horse exploded and raced around the corral in full bucking mode. Mister Jacobs and Bill watched as he twisted in mid-air, heaving Edgar out of the saddle. The man fell with a deathly thud to the ground while the wild stallion ran off, still bucking the saddle. Edgar got up slowly and dusted himself off. "Had to happen."

"I think we're done for the day," Mister Jacobs said.

"Never leave a horse half-broke," Edgar reminded the older man. He rubbed his back and massaged his arms for a minute. "I'll give him one more try." He lassoed the animal and brought him close enough to grab the reins. Then he was in the saddle again. They made almost a half-circle of the corral before Edgar hit the dust again. "Damn, that hurt." Edgar limped to the fence.

"My turn?" Bill said the words doubtfully.

"The hell it is!" Mister Jacobs said.

"You said I was a natural." Bill's pride wouldn't let him back off, but he wasn't going to press the issue anymore.

"Yeah, but this ain't just a regular horse," Mister Jacobs said.

"I don't cotton to getting on him again, but he's still only half broke at best." Edgar hugged himself and gritted his teeth. He took the rope out and lassoed the horse once more. He looked over at Bill. The temptation was strong to pass this ride on to the younger man. The big horse's head was high. The ears were back, and the eyes wild.

Bill felt the dread rise up in his belly. He saw Edgar's glance toward him and wished he had kept his mouth shut. He knew a tumble could hurt bad. Then, unpredictably, the big Roan winked at him. That made him laugh a bit.

"Did you see that?"

"What?" Edgar said. He looked back at the animal stamping its feet impatiently, waiting to buck him off again.

"He's winking at me. He's daring me to ride him!" Suddenly, Bill felt his fear fade. His blood was up.

"No, he's not winking at you," Edgar said.

"He is! Let me have a shot!"

Edgar looked at Mister Jacobs. The older man could hear the enthusiasm in Bill's voice. The boy really wanted to give it a try. A worn-out rider is at risk on a bucking horse, and Edgar was for sure worn out. He well knew the danger.

"Youth." Mister Jacobs said the word out loud and remembered his earlier ruminations. "All right! Give him a ride!"

Bill found his legs quivering but with anticipation rather than fear as he approached the big horse. He searched for a sign of acquiescence, but there was none. The head was high. The ears were back and flat against the big roan's head. The eyes were unflinching. Bill belatedly wondered if the wink was a trick or just a gnat in the horse's eye. He ran his hand down the big boy's muzzle. The horse tossed it off. Bill watched the hide on the shoulders flinch. He grabbed the reins and did a half hop. Bill rammed his shoe into the stirrup and flung his leg over the roan's back.

Edgar lifted the loop. The big horse exploded. Bill had barely landed in the saddle before being flung sidewise. He landed on his butt. Instantly, adrenalin surging, Bill sprang to his feet. He jerked the reins hard and again was back in the saddle. Again, the horse leaped sidewise, but Bill was ready this time. He stood in the stirrups, and the horse did a series of straight-ahead heaving bucks. The saddle slammed against Bill's butt four times before changing rhythm and catching him on the rebound. Again, Bill hit the dirt. This time he lost the reins. He picked himself up and watched the animal continue to buck as it headed for the far side of the corral. Bill wiped the sweat from his eyes and glanced at the two men standing behind the fence.

"You done?" Edgar yelled.

"No!" Bill said.

Edgar looked at Mister Jacobs.

"Hell, give him another try," the old man said.

Edgar worked the horse side to side until he could get the rope on him again. The massive animal reared and pawed the air. Edgar brought him to earth with a snap of the rope and got him against the fence again.

Bill approached while Edgar pulled down on the rope. Bill again ran his hand down the big animal's muzzle. "Just a little ride," he whispered. "Just a little ride, you and me." He was in the saddle in a moment as Edgar removed the loop. Everyone waited. The heavily lathered horse took a tentative step forward, whirled about, and headed full-gallop toward the far end of the corral. Bill saw the fence coming in a blur through the blinding sweat. He was sure the horse planned to slam head-on through the fence. But the animal had a different plan. Galloping full tilt, the big boy sat down on its butt at the very last moment. Bill should have gone over his shoulder. He should have landed on the fence if not over it, but he didn't. Instead, Bill flung his arms around the animal's neck, pushed the stirrups forward as hard as he could, and cried, "yee-haw" at the top of his voice. For a moment, the horse sat, butt on the ground, forelegs braced just inches from the fence. Then he righted himself and snorted before turning and, with Bill sitting tall in the saddle, returned to the men behind the fence.

"Dang," Edgar said.

"What do you call that?" Mister Jacobs said.

"That was something," Edgar said.

"Get off that horse, boy, before he changes his mind," Mister Jacobs laughed. "You've done bored him to a standstill. You keep that up, and we'll be calling you Bronco Brumley! Boy, that was something! Wasn't that something, Edgar?"

Edgar rubbed his sore shoulders with his blistered hands. He ached in every joint. "That was something all right." He limped across the lot and enjoyed a private smile. Someday soon, maybe he wouldn't have to be the first rider in the bronco riding rotation?

THE END

Sarge, ON A SEARCH FOR THE CALICO CAT

"I think Callie is missing," Brownie said. It was a pleasant late Sunday afternoon in August. Men from the neighboring farms were arriving for a meeting in the big farmhouse's extensive library. The two ten-year-old boys, Madison Jones and his black friend, Brownie, knew that the informal get-together would last at least an hour. Madison's older brother, Tom, would attend. Even at a young age, Tom was already a tall, lean, powerful young man. For a moment, Madison considered finding a place in the corner of the room to camp out and listen in. It was interesting to listen to their neighbors' colorful language as they complained about commodity prices, told stories, and joked with one another. He didn't realize it, but sometimes they would eye the boys in the middle of a joke and make the punchlines a bit less graphic.

Brownie had been born on the neighboring, Ingerstall farm. He got his name from the Mister himself, according to Ingerstall's old black slave, Isiah. "Dark chocolate with just a touch of cream," the old man had intoned.

After pointing out that Callie, their Calico cat, seemed to be missing, the black boy looked at his friend quizzically. With the mystery of the missing cat posed in front of him, Madison read the dark eyes and discarded the idea of sitting in with the men. Finding Callie seemed more interesting than the meeting and was something they could do together. The negro boy, being black, was not considered a suitable attendee of the white men's meetings. Brownie knew that and could have resented it a little, even though it was not on the top of his list of ways to spend his Sunday afternoon.

Since his purchase from the neighboring Ingerstall farm a year and a half before, the two boys, so close in age, had become fast friends. They were rarely apart other than when Madison was at school. The school was not offered for black children, so at Mrs. Jones's insistence, Madison went over his lessons with Brownie every evening after his classes were over. Brownie, quick and curious, always had questions. Figuring out the answers forced Madison to absorb more learning than he might have on his own.

"Let's search the house first," Madison said. The boys started in the large parlor with the oil portrait of Madison's mother over the fireplace. Looking under and around the furnishings, they called out the cat's name, "Callie, Callie." Before the farmer's meeting, the front door was held open with a doorstop, and the arriving men knew to go on around the corner directly into the library. Madison's mother used another area immediately off the parlor, toward the back of the house, for a sewing room. They found her there.

"Mother, we think Callie is missing," Madison said as they joined her.

"Well, I'm sure she will turn up." Mrs. Jones sat regally in a rocking chair. She was a pretty woman of fair complexion and silken brown hair. She sat near a window to catch the breeze and the light. She looked at the two boys with affection. There was little formality about the Jones farm. The most elaborate social functions involved church activities at the Baptist and Methodist churches in Titustown.

It was her habit to recluse herself when her husband, John, was entertaining friends. She put refreshments out beforehand, and when the voices grew louder as the men began to pass through the parlor on their way home, she would come out of her room and call out for them to pass on her good wishes to their spouses.

Many cats were frequenting the barns and storage sheds. They were the first line of defense against rats, mice, and other small unwelcome critters. Callie held a special place in the animal hierarchy as the only feline allowed to come into Mrs. Jones' house. The tri-colored black, white and fawn animal caught Mrs. Jones' fancy as a kitten. The cat settled with her bed close to the fireplace in the parlor and prowled the house for unwelcome critters and warmer accommodations on cold winter evenings.

The boys retreated from the sewing room and passed the library door where John Jones entertained his visitors. People said it was the most comprehensive library in the county, with bookshelves on all four walls. The bookcases even surrounded a pair of exterior windows opened to the front porch and edged to within a few feet of the entry door. Smoke from a half dozen fragrant pipes already created a gray haze. Callie avoided large crowds, so the boys barely gave the library a passing glance. Instead, they hurried to the next doorway and entered Madison's parent's bedroom.

They were still calling for Callie as they entered. Madison knelt to look under the bed, for the cat sometimes liked to conceal herself. Brownie looked behind the twin chairs. They could hear the booming voice of one of the men from the room next door. The bed-chamber, like the library, featured bookcases of dark stained burled walnut on the shared wall. The bookshelves were sectioned into four seven-foot-high by four-foot-wide components. Arising from his knees, Madison realized something he had never noticed before. In the narrow space on one side of a section of shelves, the voices from the other room seemed louder than anywhere else. Madison called Brownie over.

"Listen!"

Brownie joined him, and they looked at each other in surprise. "Why can we hear better here than here?" Madison stepped back to the far side of the adjoining bookcase.

Brownie's brow furrowed. "That is right strange." He put his ear to the narrow gap between the bookcases and slowly dropped to his knees as he followed it to the floor. Eventually, he lay with his cheek against the hard surface and pointed. "They's little wheels under these shelves."

Madison dropped to look. "They's wheels under this end of the shelf but not on the other!" Madison said as he pushed the shelf hard. It seemed to move, but so little that he couldn't be sure. He pushed harder. It did move a bit and then returned to its original position, for it was laden with books. "It does move!"

Brownie grasped the other end and pushed, then pulled. There was no perceptible movement. "Why is them wheels under a bookshelf?" He tilted his head and looked at Madison curiously. Madison pushed and then, on impulse, grasped the bottom shelf and pulled it toward him. It resisted, but he motioned for Brownie to help, and between them, they could draw it out half an inch. The rollers gave a little squeak.

The boys braced themselves and pulled together. The shelf moved another inch, then two. They could tell now that it hinged to the wall on the end opposite the rollers. Behind the shelving section, separated by a void the thickness of the wall, was the back of a bookshelf in the library. The voices were quite clear now. With a mighty tug, the boys pulled the end of the bookcase another two feet so that Brownie could kneel in the opening. He pressed his eye against the crack between the shelves in the library. There, centered in the space, was the side of Mr. Ingerstall's head. Brownie's eyes widened, and he jumped back. Mister Ingerstall was his old owner, the man who had sold him to the Jones family when he was eight years old. Brownie once told Madison that there was something creepy about the old man. Brownie carried the unspoken fear that having sold him, he could take him back if he decided he wanted to. Every time he encountered the man from time to time in town or traveling by in his wagon, this fear weighed on him. Strangely,

Mister Ingerstall never acknowledged him. It seemed he was invisible. It was the seeming invisibility that annoyed him. But at the same time, it eased his fear of someday being forced to return.

Thrilled at their discovery of a "secret door," the boys pushed the bookcase back flush against the wall and lit out at a run to Mrs. Jones's sewing room.

"Mother, they's a secret door in your bedroom!" Madison's eyes were big. His mother glanced at him then into the equally lively black eyes of Brownie.

"Son, 'they's' is terrible grammar. You should say, "there is," not 'they's." She took off her thimble and lay it aside. There was amusement in her correction. "Silly boys! It's not a secret door. Years ago, when you were but a baby, your father ran out of book space. So he had bookcases installed in the doorway between our bedroom and the library."

"Oh." Madison dropped to the floor and looked up at her. "So, everyone knows about it?"

She saw a look of disappointment on the boys' faces. "Well, everyone who was ever in the library before he added the bookshelves, I suppose. I suspect they probably forgot about it after all this time, though, don't you?" She smiled. "Okay, let's pretend it is a secret, shall we?" Her eyes changed to reflect an air of mystery for a moment before she switched the subject. "Have you found Callie yet?"

Reminded of their mission, the boys leaped up and searched the remaining three bedrooms—still no Callie.

Madison and Brownie abandoned the house to search the big barn. The sound of their calling aroused several barn cats. They came eagerly, tails high, and twined through the boys' legs as they walked through the stalls and watched with interest as they climbed into the barn loft.

Finding nothing in the loft, the boys continued their search. The hens in the chicken yard clucked a welcome as they passed on their way to the implement shed. They found Callie then. She was nesting under the wagon's seat on a burlap sack, and five kittens were tugging at her underside. The boys gave Callie a few soft strokes and touched the little kittens for a few minutes. They counted two kittens with white with black markings and two with fawn. And, most exciting, there was one calico kitten. They headed back to the house to report.

The farmers were coming out of the house and mounting their horses as the boys approached. Three men exchanged a few words before thrusting their feet into the stirrups. As two of the men mounted, the boys saw that the remaining man was Mister Ingerstall. Catching sight of them, the elderly man delayed for a moment and walked his horse a few steps in their direction. He held up his hand as if to bid them linger.

The two boys stopped, perplexed by his action. His eyes seemed stern; his mouth set until he spoke. "You boys behaving?" Though he said 'boys,' he was looking at Brownie.

"Yes, sir," they chimed together.

He pursed his lips. It was a severe yet less than threatening look. "Good, see that you do." He reached out as if to touch the black boy's head but let his hand fall to his side. "You happy here, boy?"

Brownie swallowed, and his eyes grew big. The words touched on his greatest fear. He looked at the stern mouth and then the hand that had almost reached out to him. He glanced sideways at Madison, and his chin dodged downward as if to avoid eye contact. "Yes, sir."

"Good, you boys go on and play." Mister Ingerstall turned away and mounted his horse. He neither looked back nor waved as he rode from the yard.

"Let's go tell mother," Madison said.

For a moment, Brownie searched his friend's face. He wondered what they should say. Would she be upset or angry at the man's odd behavior? How could he describe the eyes, the set of the mouth, the sternness in the voice? The man's questions tugged at his memory of Isiah's explanation for his name. For the first time, Brownie wondered why Mister Ingerstall was the one to name him rather than his now-deceased mother.

"I'll bet she'll be excited to know about the kittens, especially the calico," Madison said. He grinned and lit out for the house at a run.

Brownie shifted his train of thought away from the gruff old man with a shake of his head and followed. He realized that Mister Ingerstall's words, though chilling to him, were already forgotten by his friend. Madison was full of the news about the kittens. Brownie forced this new puzzle aside. He would ponder it on another day.

THE END

Preacher, ON THANKFULNESS

Robert Gracey stood at the pulpit and looked out over the congregation of the First Street Baptist Church in Pumpkin, Missouri. He was twenty years old. He was of modest height but big of head, girth, and heart.

Every Sunday, Robert read a passage of scripture to introduce the pastor's sermon. It was part of his several years-long understudy work with the Reverend Samuel Dickson, who was sitting on the dais behind him. As a result, Robert was pretty comfortable speaking publicly. Recently, in addition to the morning service scripture reading, he had begun to present a short sermon for the Sunday evening service. He lifted his head as he announced the selection. "The scripture this morning is *Psalms 28:7* if you would like to read along."

He opened the Bible at the ribbon bookmark and tapped the page with his forefinger. The book's onionskin paper adhered to the tip of his finger, and he was glad that he would not need to turn the page to read the required scripture.

He paused while people thumbed through their Bibles. Baptists brought their Bibles to church, for they liked to follow along with the scripture reading. It was a Baptist tradition. After a moment's lull, Robert began to read, "*The Lord is my strength and my shield; in him my heart trusts, and I am helped; my heart exults, and with my song, I give thanks to him.*"

Robert's face glowed a bit with a sense of satisfaction, for he read with a soaring voice that neither stumbled nor stammered. He closed the Good Book, looked at the congregation, and his lips parted, revealing his big wide, gap-toothed smile.

Only then did he glance for but a second at Miss Carrie Carlton. She was sitting in the third row with her parents, John and Mary Carlton, and her younger brother, Darrell. Admiring her from the pulpit, Robert again realized that he cared a great deal about how the young lady felt about him.

Though Robert approached his Sunday morning contribution with great reverence, there was also an element of performance. He felt that he acquitted himself well. Carrie's father, Mister Carlton, was one of the most prosperous farmers in the county. He was said to be a good man. Robert spoke with him, but briefly, at social gatherings in the offhand way people talk about trivial matters. Just then, included in Robert's field of vision, were both parents whose faces held bland, noncommittal expressions. Robert intended to speak with John Carlton that day about something significant. Robert narrowed his gaze to Carrie. She was smiling the friendly, open smile that always lifted him. He loved her smile, for there was no hint of guile hiding there. Robert took a step back and turned toward the Reverend Dickson, who had already risen to approach the pulpit.

Robert received a friendly pat on the shoulder that said "well done" as the two passed. The Reverend Dickson was a slender, well-intentioned man of fifty-five years.

Robert tried not to gawk at Carrie while the preacher spoke. He knew that his admiration of the girl would show on his face. The minister's voice had a humming undertone that reminded him of a purring cat. It was not unpleasant, but the rousing music at the end of his sermons did sometimes surprise the heavy-lidded members of his flock.

When Robert was sixteen, he had told the pastor about his inclination to do the Lord's work. The minister counseled him to study and leave his senses open for the Lord's continuing call. "You are a young man yet. There is no reason to hurry. Remember what the scriptures say, *"For yet a little while, and he that shall come will come, and will not tarry."*

After the service, Robert joined the congregants in the churchyard and approached Carrie and her parents. He dutifully shook the father's hand, smiled at the mother, and turned to grin at the girl. She was eighteen years of age, pretty, a bit coltish, and not in the least shy.

"May I come by and take you for a ride after dinner, Miss Carrie?"

"I will be insulted if you don't," she said. It had become a Sunday ritual for them for better than a month.

"Well, the very last thing I want to do is insult you!" Robert's big grin moved from her to her parents. Their expressions remained friendly yet noncommittal. They knew Robert to be a respectful young man. He was a hard worker and self-educated beyond many of his contemporaries. Robert assumed that his ongoing participation in services signaled his future career intentions, but if the parents construed any particular intent from his church activities, they did not reveal it. It was enough that he came from good people who owned a reasonably successful farm and blacksmith shop on the edge of town.

"Shall I pick you up at three then?"

"Darrell and I will be ready," she said, looking at her parents and her eight-year-old brother. She was permitted time with a suitor when accompanied by Darrell, who was at an age when he was game for just about anything.

Robert's decision regarding Carrie weighed heavy on his thoughts as he joined his family for the ride home. That afternoon's outing with Carrie would be unlike any other that they had shared before, for Robert intended to propose marriage. He and Carrie did not usually spend their time together discussing weighty matters. Robert knew how to make girls laugh, and he habitually devoted himself to that endeavor at the expense of serious discussion. The subject of love between the couple seemed elusive other than in a playful way. The approaching conversation was going to be as different as any could be.

After lunch, Robert returned to the church and secured the team outside. He opened the unlocked door and slid into the back pew. Over the five years since Robert felt his first religious calling on a balmy summer evening under the canopy of stars, prayer had become a solace for him. In the year since he began his official spiritual training with Reverend Dickson, he often sat and looked up at the chancel and absorbed the Presence as he came to consider it. It was a small church. There was no organ, nor did stained-glass figures depicting biblical stories adorn the windows. Instead, the glass was tinted yellow, giving the room an unusual sunrise glow even on cloudy days.

The pastor was going away to tend to the affairs of his elderly parents. While explaining his coming absence, he assured Robert that though study and learning would always be an on-going part of his life as a preacher, he had progressed enough to assume responsibility for a month while the older man was away. After accepting the preacher's expression of confidence, Robert's prayer on this occasion dealt not with his preparedness for his duties with the church but his readiness to ask first Carrie and then her father for her hand. Robert knew that the words he chose to express his commitment to Carrie and their life together were important.

Robert bowed his head and cleared his mind of all except his coming discussion with Carrie. He considered the light-hearted character of their relationship. A proposal was a serious matter. But, of course, she would say yes! After a half-hour of prayer and strategizing, Robert climbed into the wagon for the two-mile ride to the Carlton farm.

Robert continued to ruminate on his plans along the way. Daisies were everywhere, so he stopped to pick a bouquet. When he arrived, Robert grinned as he pretended to hand the flowers to his prospective father-in-law, who snorted and called on his young son to fetch his sister. As usual, Mrs. Carlton came in behind Carrie and instructed her to wear her bonnet to prevent freckling.

Since Robert had important things to discuss with the young lady, he drove the wagon to a rocky beach along the river where Darrell could amuse himself skipping rocks on the water and building castles in the sand. Robert kicked himself for forgetting to bring a fishing pole and a few worms. The boy, while distractible, had a short attention span. That fact acted as an incentive to begin his pursuit quickly.

The conversation was light-hearted as they made their way to the bank of the stream. Finally, they deposited a blanket in the shade of a swaying willow, and young Darrell departed to play along the bank of the lazy river.

"Carrie, I have something I want to talk with you about," Robert began. His heartbeat increased.

The pretty girl glanced at Robert as if she expected him to say something charming or funny. "Okay."

"I think that we get along very well, don't you?" Robert's eyebrows went up.

"Of course," Carrie said. She held down the edge of her skirt as a breeze kicked up.

"I think that since I've completed my training and will be covering for Reverend Dickson while he is away, that maybe we should think about getting married."

"Oh?" Carrie's demeanor suggested that marriage was not a subject that she had considered very much.

"Well, we do get along. You know that I have feelings for you."

"Yes." She looked at him from the corner of her eye, then turned to face him. "And you do have a farm, and I'm a farm girl," Carrie said the words as if fitting a piece of an imaginary jigsaw puzzle into place.

"Well, I probably won't be a farmer," Robert said. "I like farming, but I think that I want to be like the apostles in the

Bible and be a fisher of men." He grinned at the comparison until he saw her lips remain impassive. He realized that she did not recognize the reference. Robert continued. "You know I've been studying with Reverend Dickson to enter the ministry for a full year now."

"Yes, you have been helping out at church, but I thought you are going to be a farmer." Carrie's eyes studied him.

"That isn't my calling," Robert said soberly. In the silence that followed, he realized how unprepared he was and how unprepared their relationship was for him to broach this subject with the girl. He studied her in a new way. She was altogether charming. The flaxen hair was a bit mussed from removing the bonnet. The perfect skin, beautiful mouth, and sky-blue eyes were unchanged. She was, after all, eighteen, he argued to himself. But Carrie was, he realized, a young eighteen. The soft hands did chores but had never struggled. She had a life of few tears. Although she moved on from playing with dolls to more adult activities, her eyes perhaps glazed over occasionally while Reverend Dickson preached. He realized that he had been too smitten to evaluate the implications of that. She looked away for a moment, her face still as she watched a cloud formation move across the sky. It was apparent that some things were also becoming clear to her.

"So, you're saying that you want to be a full-time preacher?" She turned her head and looked at him skeptically.

"Yes," Robert said. He watched as she sifted through the meaning of that as it applied to the life he offered.

"I'm a farmer's daughter. I always thought I'd marry a farmer."

"Alright," Robert said.

"I should marry a farmer, shouldn't I?"

"But you don't have to," Robert hastened to assure her. "You can do whatever you want." Robert wondered if she understood that. He questioned if her reluctance to join him in a perfectly respectable career was due to his pending profession or a lack of conviction about loving him. "I love you, Carrie." He paused and studied her face.

"Well, I love you too, but then I'd be a preacher's wife, wouldn't I?" Her voice trailed off. "I have always thought I'd marry a farmer. That seems natural, don't you think?"

"I suppose so," Robert said, feeling some resignation setting in. "Though you don't have to," he assured her again.

"Oh, but I want to! Not right now, but someday." With that, she donned the bonnet and tied the ribbons under her chin before she got to her feet.

"Darrell, it's time to go." She called to her brother. She watched Robert stand and start to fold the blanket.

"Already?" The boy approached.

"Yes, I think so. Go get in the wagon." She turned to Robert. "I like you very much, Robert. I could marry you. But I can't marry into something I don't want to be."

"Don't want to be?" He stared at her uncomprehendingly.

"I don't want to be a preacher's wife." She looked away. "All of that mealy-mouth religious talk all the time, and having to be nice to mean people. I don't want that! No, I don't want to be a preacher's wife!"

Robert helped her board the wagon, and they watched the horses plod their way to the Carlton farm in silence, as each considered the future without the other. Then, finally, he helped the girl down at her front porch.

"I hope you understand," Carrie said solemnly, with a tone of finality.

"Yes, I think I do." Robert climbed aboard the wagon and settled a little as he spoke to the horses. For a bit, Robert pondered how he could go about changing Carrie's mind, for he was sure he could woo her into accepting his proposal. Robert knew that men often won women's hearts with gifts and such. He was a good talker. He could talk her into marrying him! But as the miles slowly passed, another notion slowly came over him. He remembered the morning's scripture. *The Lord is my strength and my shield; in him my heart trusts, and I am helped; my heart exults, and with my song, I give thanks to him.*"

Robert felt his resolve to mount a campaign to court Carrie fade. He suddenly realized that he had just escaped the burden of an unhappy wife. Though he felt hurt that she so decisively rejected his calling and rebuffed him, there was more to consider. There were many kinds of gifts to be received in life. He always felt that knowing what he wanted to do with his life was a gift from God. Then in a moment of mindfulness, Robert realized that recognizing what you don't want is a gift as well. God's gift to Carrie was her self-awareness. Robert realized then that Carrie's gift of knowing what she didn't want was a gift for him as well. As he approached his father's farm, he slipped that newfound knowledge into his growing storehouse of things for which to be thankful.

THE END

Emmy, LUCKY STAR

Emmy stood beside Roger's body in the doctor's office and wondered if there were enough tears in the world to express her anguish. Her betrothed, Roger Davis, lay still on the raised table. His usually florid face atop his tall, wide-shouldered body was unnaturally still, unnaturally gray. And blood! Emmy had never seen so much blood.

Only minutes before, Roger's friend, Cal Jordon, had awakened Emmy from a deep slumber. Cal was a big young man, hefty, and capable.

"There's been an accident, Miss Emmy!"

Emmy had stood in the doorway of her little house on Pepper Street and tried to shake sleep's cobwebs. "Accident?"

"Yes, come quick! Doc says he doesn't know how much time is left!"

"Time left?" She shook her head, hoping she misunderstood the import of Cal's words. Accident? There were a thousand kinds of accidents. Everyone had minor accidents. But Cal wouldn't have come for her over a minor accident. She tried to read Cal's expression. She wished that the young man's hat didn't shade his face so much. The moonlight was meager enough without the hat. And she wished his voice didn't sound so anxious.

Cal looked down at Emmy's feet and fidgeted as he realized she was in her nightgown. His voice sounded even more strident. "Miss Emmy, put on your coat and some shoes. We need to get over to Doc's right away."

Emmy looked down at her bare feet dumbly and nodded. She turned to go into the back bedroom. From the corner of her eye, Emmy saw her ten-year-old nephew, Luke, stir on the sofa. She glanced into the first bedroom as she hurried through the house. There was a lump in the bed that she knew was her niece, Sarah. The sight of the two recently orphaned children brought that harsh reality crashing into her stream of thought. She bent down to fit the shoes on her feet. Didn't she have enough burdens already? Other questions came boiling to the surface as she rejoined Cal on the front porch.

"Tell me what happened."

"Roger is shot."

"How bad? Who shot him?"

"Bad! He shot himself." Cal grabbed Emmy's elbow to hurry her along. "We were hunting coons in the bottoms out toward Ray Carson's farm. Roger was about to take a shot, and we think he stumbled. It was dark, so we don't know for sure, but we think he must have pitched the gun away from him when he fell, and it hit on something that flipped it around. It went off when the butt hit the ground." Cal hesitated. "It's awful, Miss Emmy. It's awful!" Cal's voice almost broke with emotion.

Cal's words sent Emmy's mind racing and her feet running. Then, finally, they turned the corner from Pepper onto Main Street. Emmy shook Cal's hand from her elbow and inched ahead of him. Then Cal had to struggle to lope along fast enough to keep up. *Roger's hurt!* Cal's anxious tone had told her more than his words.

Emmy, in her panic, immediately remembered her last conversation with Roger earlier in the day. Or was it yesterday now? She didn't know what time she had awakened, and it didn't matter. Emmy noted that she and Cal were still four blocks from the doctor's office.

Roger had sought to reassure her about the two children who now slept back in her house. "Em, I'm with you whatever you decide," he had said and grinned. Emmy was not a beautiful woman, but she was pleasant-looking at forty-five years of age. She was feisty and quick-witted, and people found themselves so entertained by the expressions flitting across her face that they were not mindful of the absent beauty. Roger was taller than she. He was blond-headed with a ruddy complexion and good-humored. Then, as she and Cal continued toward the doctor's office, she remembered his eyes fastening on hers when they discussed adopting the children.

"If we take in them two young'uns, we'll be starting our tavern with them already half-growed from the get-go. No waiting around for them to grow up!"

Emmy remembered smiling. She knew he was joshing her. Roger was a good teaser, and everyone liked him for it. They had viewed the two orphaned children in the front yard through the window. They belonged to Emmy's younger sister and brother-in-law, Nancy and George Tyson. The loss of the children's mother and father to malaria had filled Emmy with the kind of despair that she had never experienced before. The parents had been stricken with fever and chills while on a trip to Savannah. The outbreak was city-wide, and thousands had died. The disease had taken them so swiftly that the news sucked all of the air from Emmy's lungs when word came.

Emmy's biggest problem until then had been deciding on the pattern to use for her wedding dress. After the parent's funeral, Emmy had talked with her betrothed about the children. She had considered that if only she and Roger had a few years of marriage behind them, maybe it would be easier. She and Roger would be settled and more confident with each other. How much easier if they already had children of their own! They'd just tuck the two new ones into the fold and go on as usual. There were many "ifs," and Emmy was very unsure of any decision she might make. She loved both of the children. She had looked after them from infancy. They were happy and resourceful by nature. Even now, they distracted themselves from their terrible loss rather than moping about it. At least there'd be no diapers to change! She had smiled at that. It was the kind joke that Roger would make. Her decision was an important one.

"Roger, I don't feel like it's a decision, really." She had looked into his eyes, trying to see a hint of his real feelings. Sometimes, Roger hid what he actually thought about things to please people. Emmy didn't want to start their marriage out on that foundation. She didn't want to catch Roger looking at her or the two children and see regret in his eyes. But, as she had just said, it didn't seem like a decision between two things. There was only one way to bring some solace to her heart.

Roger had looked back at her soberly as if he suddenly realized the magnitude of her concern that he agreed. He had taken her hands and bowed toward her so that his forehead touched hers. He had looked her square in the eyes.

"I want us to adopt them two, Em. I do." His big hand tipped up her chin, and he kissed her. Emmy felt a flood of gratefulness fill her heart. She wondered again as she often did how she was so lucky to be marrying such a good-hearted man.

"Those," she said. "We want to adopt those two." She had smiled, watching him grin at her corrective words.

"Okay, you can adopt those two, and I'll adopt them two, and we'll for sure have it covered," he said. "No matter what happens, we'll work it out!" Then he had grinned again. Emmy remembered her thankfulness that the terrible loss of her sister could not extinguish the promised future with Roger.

Cal and Emmy approached a nearly completed building. Emmy scarcely looked at it, but again her mind sought solace from her present fear to her memories of Roger.

This enterprise was a small six-room hotel and tavern that would serve food and drink to the guests and travelers who traveled through Harlon County. In addition, the new location for the livery stable would be convenient for guests in their hotel. Two decades earlier, the gold boom in the nearby hills had brought in many able-bodied men who had bought up the land roundabout after their placer mining success. The gold had played out, but small farms now dotted the valleys and foothills of northwest Georgia. Slowly the town had grown as it acquired a general store, a dry-goods store, and a feed store. Eventually, a bank followed. Next, there were Methodist and Baptist churches.

"I know what I want to name it." Roger had told her. He looked down at the diminutive Emmy and waited.

"Oh, What?" Emmy had sensed the excitement in Roger's voice. He had always found it easy to infect her with his enthusiasm for his varied projects.

Emmy and Cal were approaching the doctor's office. The young man was matching her step for step. She could hear his breath coming in gasps that echoed her own. But Roger was still in her thoughts.

"Remember the night I proposed to you?" Roger looked away from the building.

Emmy had nodded. She smiled. "I'm not likely to ever forget that." She had pulled his upper arm more snuggly against her bosom and waited for him to continue.

"Well, you were sitting in the wagon. I was standing on the ground looking up to you."

"That's the only way you could ever look up at me!" Emmy laughed.

"True. Anyway, I noticed just as you said "yes" that the North Star came out from behind a cloud. It was shining about an inch above your head."

Emmy had nodded. "Let me guess. You think we should name the new business North Star!" She cocked her head back in triumph.

"Nope." Roger shook his head. "We should name it the Lucky Star."

"I think you kissed the Blarney Stone," Emmy had laughed. She could not imagine being any happier with him.

Emmy and Cal were well past the new building, now, and rounded the corner. Her eyes caught very briefly on the doctor's shingle. *Phillip Jenkins, M.D.* Cal's big hand reached in front of her, and the door swung in. No one had lit a light in the small waiting room. Emmy knew that hidden in deep shadow; six chairs lined the walls. She knew the hall to the treatment room was straight ahead toward the light. She steeled herself. The door to the chamber was open. Cal let her go first, and Emmy took a deep breath and stepped inside. Two other young men awaited them with the doctor; Pappy Jordon's son, Howie, and Tom Jones. Their heads all jerked around at her appearance. They stiffened for a moment; then, in unison, all eyes turned back toward the man lying on the high table. Doctor Jenkins was standing nearby.

Emmy could feel her heart thudding in her chest from the run, but it redoubled as she hurriedly approached the blond-headed man who reclined there.

"Roger?" The ghastly sight stunned her. Emmy could see the blood-matted blond hair. Roger's eyelids were closed at first, but he turned his head when he heard her voice. Emmy grabbed his hand.

"I'm right sorry, Em," he gasped. He coughed, and a little blood came with the words that followed. "I think I'm a goner, but I want you to go ahead and open the tavern. Take the money we have saved at the bank and go to it."

She rebelled at the idea that he thought he was dying. "I don't want your share, Roger. I want you!" She said it as a kind of command. She didn't want to hear final words or for any witnesses to listen to them. Emmy glanced around the tiny room. It seemed to her that the more people who heard his words, the more likely they would come true.

Roger coughed again, and Cal stepped over to drape a towel over Emmy's shoulder to cover her bosom for protection from the blood. She unconsciously smoothed it with her free hand, unmindful of its purpose.

Roger's eyes seemed to glaze over then. His little panting breaths suddenly ceased. She waited for the longest moment for his breathing to resume. Then, determined, Emmy tightened her grip on his hand and shook it a little as one might try to awaken someone sleeping. When there was no response, Emmy's stricken face returned to the doctor. "He's not breathing! Make him breathe!"

"I'm sorry, Miss Emmy." Doctor Jenkins reached over to close the eyelids. "He was just hurt too bad."

"Let me take you home, Ma'am," Cal said. He took a step toward Emmy.

"I'm not ready!" Her legs stiffened as if to resist any attempt to remove her from the room.

"Let's leave her here for a minute." Doctor Jenkins waved Tom and the two cousins toward the door.

Emmy looked at the blood-spattered cloth covering Roger's chest. She dabbed at the hated blood on Roger's mouth and chin. The damaged chest lay bare through the tatters of his shirt. She pulled the clean cloth that Cal had placed on her shoulder, covered the bloodied chest, and then sank in a chair to study Roger's profile. She didn't know if she was strong enough to survive this.

First her sister and now the person she loved most in all the world? "It's too much!" She stood again and shook Roger's arm. "It's too much!" Emmy stared at the still face. In just a few minutes, it seemed as if the big blond man had shrunk in size. Was that what happened when the soul departed? Was a man's soul a physical thing that left them hollow and shrunken when it left? She had never heard of that. She couldn't recall any preacher explaining that. But here it was. It was clear as day. Why was she the only one to notice that?

Even amid her thoughts about souls and immortality, a part of Emmy clung to the belief that Roger wasn't really dead. It wasn't possible. She remembered when they had stood together in front of the near-completed building on Main Street. She remembered their grand plans. Then she wept again.

They held the funeral two days later. Emmy stood at the gravesite after everyone left and ran through all of the recent events once again. The earth was still fresh over her sister and brother-in-law's graves. Now, this. But she could not dwell too closely on the details. The despair would swallow her if she did. Young Cal Jordon approached. She turned away toward the road and allowed him to lead her to the wagon. Off in the middle distance, she could see her niece and nephew wander across the yard together. Their heads tilted downward, and every so often, one would kneel and separate a four-leaf clover from its three-leaf companions and hold up the trophy with an expression of satisfaction. She was glad they were so resilient. She called them, and they climbed into the back of the wagon. Cal called to the horses, and the wagon lurched forward down the lane to the road. Everything passed in a haze until they pulled up in front of the new hotel building that Roger had planned so meticulously.

Cal looked at her. "Maybe this isn't a good time to bring it up, but some of the fellas were asking in case they needed to look for other work. Do you know what you're going to do with that?"

"Yes, I do," Emmy said.

"Oh?"

"Yes, I'm going to finish it. I'm going to open it and run it just as if Roger was still here."

"You're sure?"

"Yes, and I'm going to call it the Lucky Star! It was Roger's plan, and I'm going to see it through."

Cal looked perplexed. "Why Lucky Star?" Emmy knew that he could see nothing lucky about the recent events.

"Because meeting Roger Davis was the luckiest thing that ever happened to me." She turned toward Cal. "He will always be my lucky star."

THE END

Bronco, DAY OF THE RIFLE

Bronco Brumley threw his leg over the neck of the black mustang and slipped down the fender to land on his two feet in the dusty corral. He reached around to stroke the head of the big animal he had just ridden to a standstill. The stallion tossed his head and snorted to prove he might be tired but not beaten. Bronco stepped away and laughed.

"Don't go snorting in my ear, big boy!"

Bronco, a seventeen-year-old small-town boy, had never been astride a horse until he arrived at the Jacobs' horse training farm. His grandfather had died, and the young man needed work. The elderly Sam Jacobs, who owned the farm, had hired him on the spot despite his slight build.

It was 1863, and with the war on, he had few able-bodied prospects. The hiring turned into a godsent to the old man and his middle-aged foreman, Edgar Andrews. Farm chores muscled up Bill, and he became a steady hand. More importantly, he turned out to have extraordinary coordination and balance.

Every three or four months, a shipment of wild mustangs arrived from the western frontier. The period between shipments was busy with bone jolting work preparing the horses for service to the Union cause. No one in Pickaway County could ride a horse like Bill. Mister Jacobs started telling everyone that Bill stuck to the saddle like a fly on a cow patty. Both of the older men were well past their days when leaping on a wild horse was a thrill and a challenge. Almost immediately, Bill earned the name Bronco Brumley.

"Another day behind us." Edgar watched as Bronco unsaddled the animal and walked with him to let the newly broken horse free in the pasture.

"Yep." Bronco grinned and swung his muscled shoulders left to right to stretch his back. His hair was a curly brown and stuck out a couple of inches from under his grandfather's old hat. He was slim-waisted, with broadening shoulders, and almost six feet tall. He had a ready smile and a relaxed disposition. He was good-looking enough to turn heads among the young girls when he made an infrequent trip to town.

The men headed toward the house. Their stroll across the barnyard was interrupted by a mounted neighbor, who reined in and circled the horse about to face them.

"How are you, Jeb?" Edgar reached up to shake the rider's hand.

"Not so good. You boys had any problems with wild hogs messing with your stock?"

"Don't think so." Edgar's eyes swept the near pasture as if to reassure himself.

"Well, they took down one of my ewes and made a mess of her."

"That so? You know we had a bunch of them around here about ten years ago. The sheriff organized a hunt, and we shot a dozen of them in all. Haven't seen any since."

Jeb pulled off his bandana and mopped his deeply tanned face and neck. "I'm going to talk with the sheriff and see if anyone else has had trouble." He waved and reined the horse around to head on into Ashville.

"Well, let us know what you find out," Edgar called after him.

"Hogs?" Bronco eyed the older man. Edgar glanced at Bronco.

"Ever done any hunting, Bill?"

"No, sir, but I'd like to try it." Bronco rubbed his chin.

"Well, feral hogs used to be a problem, but I haven't heard of any in Pickaway County in a very long time. Come on. I bet supper's waiting."

The men ascended the steps and found the farm's owner, Sam Jacobs, tending the stove. "How'd it go with that black stallion?"

"He had a mind of his own, but Bronco wore him out," Edgar said.

"Sir, that fella, Jeb Stallcup, from up the road came by and said wild hogs attacked his sheep." Bronco leaned on the back of a chair and watched the old man's expression.

"That so!" Sam pulled the skillet off the stove and divvied the meat and potatoes into the three plates laid out on the table.

"It's been a while since we've had a predator problem," Edgar said. "I bet it's been ten years since we went on our last hunt. We don't even hunt for food anymore. We've sure gotten spoiled on store-bought eats, haven't we?" He looked at Sam. "Wolves! I remember it was over in the back pasture. A pack of five wolves, I think. I plugged one with that old Brown Bess over there over the mantle. He pointed with his thumb behind him toward the fireplace.

"I remember that," Sam said and laughed. "You were almost a hundred yards away. I remember thinking, what a shot!"

"I couldn't do that again if my life depended on it," Edgar said.

"Why is that?" Bronco pulled up close to the table and reached for his fork.

"Cause old Bess has got a smooth bore," Sam said. "And there ain't no sights. So she ain't that accurate."

"The truth is, I aimed for an area about ten-foot square and got lucky." Edgar jabbed a bite of new potato into his mouth. "I probably couldn't hit the side of a barn with it now. My eyes were a whole lot better back then."

"Maybe I could give it a try?" Bronco felt his interest stir. "I've got pretty good eyes."

"Nah, forget it," Sam said. "We ain't even got powder for old Bess anymore. If you want to learn to shoot proper, you need a more modern weapon. Smooth bores are terrible for accuracy. It's best that the old Brown Bess stays right where she is. Her time is long gone."

Edgar nodded in agreement. "Wild hogs are dangerous if you get up close, especially when they're traveling in a sounder. They's fast and vicious. So if I came on a wild boar out in the woods, I'd head for the nearest tree." He grinned. "'Course then I'd have to climb it, and that day is past too!"

Bronco nodded. Still, it was exciting to think about shooting a wild boar on the run. It sounded like you needed skill for sure, even with a good weapon.

"Bronco, I want you to go into town tomorrow and pick up some vittles. We're about out of flour and oatmeal. Here's a list." Sam put the paper down next to the young man's plate. "Don't take too long. We've still got a fair number of mustangs to tame before the army procurement fella shows up again."

Early to bed and to rise, Bronco rode one of the mustangs he broke the week before into town. He handed the list to Mister Morgan, the storekeeper, and leaned back in a chair close to the potbellied stove, which was stone cold in August, while he waited. His glance around revealed some empty shelves. Bronco knew that a lot of goods had gotten diverted to the army since the war started. Then his gaze traveled to the far end of the counter. There was a row of shotguns and rifles leaning against the back of the display cabinet. He walked over.

Mister Morgan looked at Bronco out of the corner of his eye. "Got an interest in a long gun, son?"

"Well, sir, I might." Bronco leaned over the counter for a better look. "What would you reckon a good one would be?"

"Well, you looking for a rifle or a shotgun?' Mister Morgan moved toward the display. He picked up one of the weapons and broke it open. Now here's a pretty good shotgun."

Bronco remembered what Sam said about a smooth bore not being very accurate. And Edgar said you didn't want to get close to one of the wild pigs. "I'm looking for a rifle."

"Ok. Let's see. Here is a Henry rifle. Lever action. Pretty accurate in the right hands." He looked Bronco up and down. "You heading out to join the army, son?" He passed the weapon across the counter.

"Well, no, sir. It would be for hunting. I work for Mister Jacobs breaking horses for the army. I'm not old enough to be drafted, and I don't expect he'd appreciate me taking off right now." Bronco put the butt of the rifle against his shoulder and squinted down the barrel.

In fifteen minutes, the purchase was complete. It took a good chunk of Bronco's inheritance money for the thirty-five-dollar Henry rifle, ammunition, saddle scabbard, and cleaning supplies. When he arrived at the farm, he lugged everything into the house and looked at the two men with a grin.

"I'll be damned," Sam said when Bronco unloaded everything on the table. "You don't let the grass grow under your feet, do you?"

"No, sir, though I might need some schooling on how to use it."

Sam looked at Edgar. "You up to that?"

Edgar stood. "After we're done with the horses this evening, let's go out to the back forty where I shot that wolf and figure that thing out. But just knowing about it won't make you a marksman. I see you bought a goodly amount of ammunition. You'll probably need it and more before you're an eagle eye."

It was six o'clock that afternoon when the three men returned from the bluff where Bronco learned about handling the rifle. The ground had washed out around the roots of a dead oak tree almost a hundred yards away. The chunk of roots made a good target. They took turns shooting up Bronco's ammunition. After passing the rifle around a few times, the older men let Bronco do all of the shooting.

"Well, that is a sweet rifle," Sam said. He limped for the first few steps after climbing off the fence.

"Having a sight sure helps with accuracy, but not enough for me," Edgar said, looking over at the older man. "Say, Bronco, I noticed that you put your last three shots in that one spot?"

"Yes, sir. That was a knot-hole." Bronco grinned.

"Well, I couldn't tell except for the fragments flying. I was right about my eyes."

"And we still have ammunition left." Bronco balanced the weapon against the far side of the split-rail fence and leaped across.

As the men crossed the pasture, they spotted a horse and rider in front of the house. "I believe that's Jeb again," Edgar said.

They picked up their pace and joined the man as he dismounted. "I talked to the sheriff yesterday. He said there had been three sightings of wild hogs in the last week. He thinks it may be as many a twenty scattered about in groups of five to ten." He looked at Bronco and his new Henry. "I heard the shooting. You boys in for the hunt next Saturday?"

"Maybe." Sam glanced at Bronco. This fella can already shoot the legs off a spider sitting in its web. He ain't had a chance at a moving target yet."

Jeb looked at Bronco and his Henry appraisingly. "Sheriff Mack said he'll keep track of sightings through Friday. Then, he wants hunters to assemble at his office at six o'clock Saturday morning. After that, we'll move out from there based on the last information we have. Bring water and something to eat on. We don't know how long this will take."

He climbed back into the saddle. "Hope to see you there, young fella." He reined his horse about and headed out.

"Suppertime!" Sam said. They headed inside. Bronco cleaned his new rifle while the old man fried up some bacon and made cornbread and beans.

Saturday morning Bronco joined about two dozen men and boys who showed up for the hunt. They followed the sheriff and his deputy about two miles out of town, where a farmer waited on his front porch. The man pointed toward a heavily treed area surrounding a creek. He mounted his horse and led the men into a stand of oak and dismounted. The sheriff took over from there.

"Men, I don't want to lose anybody in these woods from bullet wounds." The men laughed. "It's funny to joke about but serious if it happens. We're going to line up here at this end of the creek. Then we'll work our way north and around to the west, following the stream. Them hogs could be anywhere. The terrain is going to be rough going. I want you younger fellows to walk along the banks. Be careful. Remember, this ain't no race. You fellows on the outskirts where it's not so thick need to be mindful that you don't get ahead of everyone else. It's really easy to do that. If you do, then if we come to the hogs, we'll find ourselves in almost a circle around them and shooting toward each other. Let's do our best to keep the line organized. Everybody got that?" He looked around.

Two boys looked at Bronco, who was a year or so older than they. "How come you ain't down south killing Rebels?" The tallest asked. There was a sneer on his lips as he looked at his friend and back at Bronco. The younger boy nodded dismissively.

Bronco's face hardened. He eyed the two boys and hefted the Henry rifle. "I ain't been called yet."

"You look old enough. Twenty is the draft age. Besides, the government don't have to call for you to go. So I'm going next spring, and I'm only seventeen." The other boy nodded his head enthusiastically.

"Me too," he said.

"I ain't been called 'cause I ain't twenty yet. Besides, I'm breaking horses for the army." The boys made faces at each other as if the explanation was insufficient.

Bronco was about to advance another rejoinder when the conversation was interrupted by more directions from the lawman. Bronco and half a dozen men crossed to the other side of the creek and strung out fifteen to twenty feet apart. As he began to follow the stream, Bronco kept sight of the two boys. With everyone in place, the sheriff belatedly motioned for them to move out. They moved on into the woods. The creek was flowing a little, and the vegetation grew right up to the edge of the bank. The terrain alternated between descending to sandbars leading out into the water to cutaway bluffs ten to twelve feet above the creek bottom.

The two boys stayed close to each other on the right side of the stream. The sheriff shouted his final warning. "Remember, Tom Higgins saw them hogs rooting around in this area yesterday. Be careful; a boar hog is dangerous." He paused for emphasis, "especially a wounded one!"

Bronco moved along the left side. The terrain changed frequently, and the underbrush and fallen leaves made walking a tricky business. Along one tough expanse, a fallen tree delayed Bronco. He worked himself around it and came out on a sandbar. He could see the boys moving along the edge of the high bluff on the other side. He was about to shout a warning for them to take care so close to the edge when he realized, as did the young men, that there was movement below the spot where they were perched. Bronco could see a sandy wallow occupied by at least a dozen hogs in the washout directly below them. There were two sows with a half-dozen pigs each. All of their heads tilted upward in reaction to the rustling above them. Dirt and leaves drifted down from the upper bank.

One of the boys edged out on the unstable rim a bit too far; the soil crumbled. He gasped and cried out as he dropped the first several feet. The other boy flung a hand out to grab him, but the additional load on the loosened soil only made things worse.

Bronco stiffened. The first boy managed to grab the trunk of a small sapling, but it was green and not well anchored. The tree scarcely slowed his descent as it yielded to his weight and then pulled loose from the soil. The boy cried out again and clawed at the bank. Now dangling one-handed from a tangle of roots, the boy's feet were almost within reach of the boar.

The sows squealed and moved away. The boar's body tensed, and the huge animal grunted. He began popping his jaws, sharpening his long, pointed cutter teeth on the blunt upper whetters. The saliva started to get foamy and drip out of his mouth. He paced stiff-legged to the side a few feet out of the shallow water to a small sandbar and stopped. His front legs were stiff in front of him.

The last roots give way. The boy's descent was almost a dead-fall, and he landed in the shallows only yards away from the sows and piglets. Terrified, the boy turned to claw his way back up the steep bank. No sooner did the first boy land than the ground gave way beneath the second. He landed beside the first thrashing his arms and legs.

In an instant, the boar's hindquarters bulged. Bronco instinctively knew he was about to charge. He imagined the view from the two boys' position lying against the creek's bank with the angry boar within pissing distance. He brought the butt of the Henry to his shoulder and aimed for the animal's left eye. He fired, but so rapidly did the hog charge that the bullet missed the target and instead lodged in the bulge of fat just behind the animal's head with a solid thump. The impact stunned the huge animal; it stumbled a step, but it didn't drop. The boys cried in terror while Bronco levered in another round. He aimed a foot ahead of the charging boar and fired again. There was another thump as the bullet found the softer tissue of the eye and sent up a red mist. The big boar's front legs buckled, and he fell snout first into the shallows. A back leg twitched twice. The boys rushed past the dead mound as Bronco approached.

Both boys had lost their weapons sliding down the bank. Bronco passed close to the ugly boar's still carcass and picked up the two old Brown Besses a few feet from the big animal's head. He handed the two ancient weapons back to the boys. With heads down and almost inaudible murmurs of thanks, the boys looked at Bronco with a bit more respect. He hefted the Henry confidently as several other men approached.

Then fear replaced the boys' rueful expressions. Bronco heard an angry grunt. The two boys took off at a run, and Bronco turned his head to look behind him. A second younger boar stood a few feet away, stiff-legged, tusks flashing. It took a tentative step forward as the foam began to drip.

Bronco had no chance to decide to run or stay and fight. Turning, he tripped on a piece of driftwood and fell awkwardly on his hip and shoulder as the boar charged. Bronco's blood turned to ice. Instinctively he rolled to the side. The boar was twenty feet away as Bronco levered the Henry. A full roll brought them face-on. Bronco's elbows sank in the soft sand; the rifle jammed against his shoulder. The boar, with tusks flashing, was almost on him. Bronco fired at the large menacing head. He spun to the side again as the animal's momentum carried it onward. Bronco felt the boar's bristles brush his shoulder as it plowed to a stop. He stared down at the bloodied carcass as he rose and then stood panting while the boys ran back to join him.

After a few deep breaths, Bronco spoke. "Dang! That was close. You know this whole thing just goes to show you that if you boys are going south to kill them Rebels, you're for sure going to need better weapons." He gave them a sterner look. "And you're going to have to walk a lot lighter and mouth off a lot less." Then he grinned.

THE END

Sarge, PROPERTY

Madison held the reins and the black boy, Brownie, rode in the shotgun seat as the two fifteen-year-olds drove the first of two wagons to the vacant lot on the far side of Titustown, Georgia, where Angus Miller waited impatiently. The pair and Madison's nineteen-year-old brother, Tom, who followed in the second wagon, were delivering lumber to construct the Irishman's new feed store. Angus, a stout man with reddish hair held in place in the early morning breeze by a flat cap, made no effort to hide his disgust. Aside from his girth, he was handsome, though a smallish man of forty and a new arrival in Harlon County from Savannah. Angus pulled out a handkerchief as the wagons pulled up and wiped his brow and then the back of his neck.

"I've been a-waiting all morning!" He spat the words out and stuffed the rag back in his hip pocket. "The sun is halfway overhead!" He charged toward Madison's wagon from Brownie's side and looked up at the startled youngsters, almost snarling. "I've got a good mind to cancel me order!" He stamped his feet for emphasis.

"Sir," Madison looked at the man with a surprised expression. "Your order says this lumber was to be delivered tomorrow, the twenty-fifth. So we're here a day early!" He glanced back over his shoulder toward Tom as the older brother pulled up behind with his wagon.

"I wanted it today, Monday," Angus said, exasperated. He stomped his feet again in the dust.

"Sir, this is the twenty-fourth. Here is your order." Madison pulled out the sheet and handed it to Brownie to pass on. Brownie looked at it and held the paper out for the man with his left hand while pointing at the April twenty-fifth delivery date with his left. Madison knew that it just specified the date, not the day.

Miller stiffened and stepped back. He appeared dumbfounded. His features flushed red as he looked up into Brownie's solemn face and down at the black boy's finger still pointing toward the date. Then, rather than look at the paper, Miller snapped his head to the side, pulled the paper from Brownie's fingers, grabbed at the black boy's offending hand, and then slapped it away.

"Don't you go a-pointing your finger for me, you little snot-nosed bastard! Don't they teach you blacks around here the proper way to address a white man? You don't never point at nothing unless a white man tells you to!" He stomped his feet again.

From the corner of his eye, Madison saw Tom quickly jump from the second wagon. He approached the man quickly, his face displaying concern.

"What's the problem, sir?" Tom kept his tone level but looked askance into the man's face. Madison felt relief. He was confident that Tom knew how to deal with a troublesome customer. Brownie pulled himself upright to lean back against Madison with confusion and fear on his features. He had never been the target of such a blatant attack before.

"That damn black scoundrel pointed at them papers as if to say I can't read. I won't have no ignorant black pretending he can read better than me or that he has the right to point at nothing unless I say so. Where I come from, a black who doesn't know his place gets a whippin' on the spot!"

Tom glanced up at the two boys. Madison could see that his older brother was as startled as he, but he hid it better. "Sir, I'm sure Brownie meant no offense. Why the commotion?"

Tom's mollifying words seemed to have little effect on Angus. "This lumber is being delivered too late in the day." Then, without looking at it, the man pushed the paper into Tom's chest. "Me order is supposed to be delivered on Monday the twenty-fifth at a decent time to get a full day's work from me men." He pointed over his shoulder with his thumb at four young men behind him who had gathered to watch the tussle.

"Sir," Tom patiently accepted the order paper from the older man's hand and smoothed it out. He straightened it and tilted his head down as if to study it. "I read this to say delivery on the twenty-fifth, sir. Today is the twenty-fourth." He looked at Angus through his eyebrows. "We always try to make deliveries when scheduled, if not before. What say we get your order unloaded so your men can get to work?" He turned the paper toward Angus for a moment as if offering him an opportunity to examine it further. When Angus showed no inclination to do so, Tom folded it and slid it into his pocket. "Where do you want it unloaded, sir?"

"Your ignorant boy insulted me!" Angus shouted, unwilling to overlook the slight. "I'll not be taking me shipment until you give him a good whipping." He stomped his feet again.

"Sir, you'll have to talk with my father about any whipping, but I can tell you now that Brownie is more to him than mere property. I know my father will not oblige you, order or no order. If you want this lumber, you should say so." His eyes flashed. "Do you want shipment or not?" He waited for a moment. Then, when there was no immediate response, he looked up at the younger boys. "Turn your wagon around, boys. I guess we won't be delivering any lumber here." Madison hurriedly picked up the reins.

Angus turned half around. He could see that two of the newly hired men were bemused. One was grinning outright. Madison's eyes also moved from face to face. He recognized all of the young men. They were all local farmhands looking for some cash money. Madison's survey ended when his eyes fell on a lightly tanned, well-proportioned young man standing with arms crossed, expressionless until he spoke.

"We ain't getting paid if we just stand around here," Ben said curtly to the others, and then he advanced on Tom and Angus. His eyes bored into the Irishman, then turned to Tom. "How are you doing, Tom?" He slapped Tom's shoulder good-naturedly. "Mister Miller, you are new around here, so I'll try to help you out." While still a young man, Ben appeared to be several years older than Tom and carried an outsized air of authority. He wasn't as tall as Tom, but he seemed strong and agile.

"Sir, John Jones' sawmill produces the best lumber around here. We all know him well, and he will not whip that boy to get your business. These men here took off from other things to work on your job. We need to get started because I expect if we lose the day, you'll also lose your crew." He put his hands on his hips and looked from Angus to Tom and then the boys in the wagon.

"Sir, according to the order you signed, we were to make delivery tomorrow. Your lumber is here ahead of schedule," Tom said. He spread his arms to encompass himself and the two boys in the wagon, and we're here. Your crew is here. I don't know how it got dated the twenty-fifth, but it's here now. What say we get it unloaded and get your men to work?"

Madison felt a bit of relief. He had known Ben Beckett for as long as he could remember. Ben and Tom had always been good friends. Madison noted Brownie's solemn expression as he rubbed his wrist and then rebuttoned his sleeve.

But the Irishman was still simmering. He reached up and grabbed Brownie's arm. "Not before I give that boy a lickin'!" The motion was so sudden that Brownie was pulled half out of the wagon before anyone could react. Madison grabbed his friend's legs but was almost pulled from the wagon as well. Brownie would have landed upside down on the ground if Tom had not thrown out his arms and broken his fall.

Angus managed to strike Brownie with a backhanded slap across his face and then balled his fists as if readying more blows. "He has that and more coming."

Before the man could launch another blow, Madison felt his contempt at the slap overtake him. He grabbed the seat for support and gave the Irishman a solid kick to the side of his head. Angus staggered away from them and then came forward in a rush, fists poised. Tom quickly pushed Brownie back into the wagon and turned to meet the man's charge. Angus's head rammed into Tom Jones' chest. Tom's left fist made a short arc catching Angus on the side of his jaw. The older man's knees buckled for a moment, but he recovered. He appeared ready to start swinging when Ben Beckett grabbed his arms from behind.

"Sir, I think you have already outstayed your welcome in Harlan County. I 'spec you aren't going to be building anything here after this." Ben looked over his shoulder at the other young men as he released Argus. His friends nodded and began to pick up their tools.

Tom crossed his arms. "If there is fault here, it is yours, and every one of these boys knows it." He pointed at the young men preparing to leave. "My father will be fine without your business. Threatening us and injuring our property won't win you any friends or business in Harlon County."

Madison looked at Brownie, satisfied that Tom's words settled the issue. He knew his friend wasn't hurt badly except for his pride. Madison shrugged it off, gave the black boy's knee a consoling slap, and then reined the team around toward town. It seemed that everything had turned out okay. Brownie set his jaw and looked straight ahead. Most of the time, Madison knew what Brownie was thinking and feeling. But, then sometimes, as now, he didn't. Madison didn't notice Brownie's lips move to mouth the cold hard word.

"Property." Brownie looked sideways at his friend. There were some words that only a black boy could feel to his core

THE END

Preacher, SUSPICIONS

"Gunther Bauer stopped by while you were at the store." Robert Gracey strode out to meet his father as the wagon halted in front of the barn. As he approached, Robert could see two wooden boxes sitting side by side in the back along with other purchases. Both the father and son were of medium height, stocky, and fair-haired. Robert was wide-shouldered and deep-chested in his early twenties. At five feet nine inches tall, he was an inch taller than his father. He had a big head, a generous mouth, and a prominent gap between his upper teeth. He was considered good-tempered and a bit adventurous for a preacher.

"Any news?"

"He says he has a horse missing."

"Oh?" Jack shook his head. "That German fellow has the hardest time keeping up with his stock. Last month he lost a sow."

"What's in the box?" Robert hefted the end of one of the wooden boxes and dropped it with a thud.

"Well, that box holds two dozen manufactured horseshoes. There's a factory in Troy, New York. They've been making horseshoes for a while now. With arthritis in my shoulder, I'm going to give these ready-made shoes a try. After all, it's 1845, and we need to keep up with the times." He grinned, for he knew he was making an excuse. "Grab a box, and let's get them to the barn. I want to see what they look like."

Robert tipped the box and slid his fingers underneath. He lugged it into the shade of the barn and dropped it on the farrier table. Jack Gracey's place, the closest farm to town on the east edge of Pumpkin, Missouri, offered the county's only blacksmith shop.

Robert grabbed the crowbar and wedged it under the near edge of the lid. The board levered open smoothly, revealing two layers of a dozen horseshoes each, packed toe-end up.

Jack ran his fingers across a row of humps appreciatively. "Smooth as a babe's butt."

Robert lay two shoes on the table side by side. "They look just alike to me."

"Yep." Jack glanced at Robert. "So, son, what's this Sunday's sermon to be?" He grinned again, for he was proud of the young man's choice of vocation. Robert was the minister of the town's Baptist church. Young for such responsibility, he had started as an understudy, but his mentor had gone away to tend to a family matter. Robert inherited the job when the man was unable to return.

"Beatitudes." Robert smiled. "There's a lot there for folks to think about in the Sermon on the Mount. You can take the eight all together or separately or in different combinations."

"Kind of like the Ten Commandments," Jack commented. "What's Gunther's take on his missing horse? Stolen?"

"He was het up with some suspicions but has no clues. The horse was there when he went to bed and gone when he went out to the pasture this morning. He was headed for the sheriff as quick as he could get there."

"This is a small town. We know pretty much who our thieves are. Billy Barns comes to mind right away, doesn't he?" Jack glanced at Robert.

"Yeah, he does." Robert remembered several times when he had been at cross-purposes with the town ne'er-do-well as far back as their grade school years. Then Robert's eyes dropped to his scuffed and tattered footwear. He placed the two horseshoes back in the box. "Well, guess I'll go shop for some new shoes for myself. Brother Bob Thomas told me it is time." Robert patted his father's shoulder and walked toward Main Street.

"Speak of the devil," Robert mumbled under his breath. County Sheriff, Abbot Cross, a tall, thick-waisted man, had big Billy Barns backed up against his office's outside wall. Gunther Bauer was standing nearby. Even a new man in the little town like Gunther knew Billy's reputation.

"Sheriff, I don't know nothing about no horse, I swear." It was evident that the sheriff had his bluff in on the man, however big he was. Billy had a history of run-ins with the law stretching back to his school days.

"Gunther, you sure that horse isn't hiding out somewhere?" Sheriff Cross looked sidewise at the farmer.

Sheriff, that mare, she hangs around the barn most of the time. I can't think of a morning when she hasn't been out there waiting for me or why she would take off." The German's English was thick on his tongue as he looked at Billy. "I ain't got no proof, but I'd guess that girl, she had help!"

"Well, it wasn't me." Billy looked around at several onlookers as if a solution to the mystery lay somewhere else.

"There's no proof?" The sheriff looked at Gunther. Then, his gaze shifted back to Billy. "Yet." The sheriff turned toward the little German. "Give your place a good search. If you find any evidence of use, let me know." He shoved Billy roughly to the side and opened the door into his office.

Billy and the German eyed each other warily as Robert approached. Then, finally, Gunther turned away and took a couple of steps toward the Preacher. "Ja, I know he did it!"

Robert glanced from Gunther back to Billy, who appeared hesitant to walk away from the fray. Robert pursed his mouth. Gunther, a recent arrival from Germany, was a good man and a member of his congregation.

"Tell you what, Gunther. Let's go out and search your place." Robert looked at the sole suspect. "Billy, why don't you come along. The more eyes, the better." Despite his history with Billy, something about the big man's denials rang true.

Gunther looked at Robert closely. If the suggestion had come from anyone else, he would have dismissed it and refused to allow the man to join them. Instead, he shrugged.

"Let's get going." Robert lifted a leg to board the wagon and looked down at his shoes. "Searching for your horse can be the last time I wear these shoes. You've got my curiosity up."

Robert took a seat on the shotgun side of the farmer's wagon and glanced back at Billy. He waved him to join them. The big man made an agreeable motion with his hands. He climbed up to lean against the back of the seat next to a sack of feed. He seemed agreeable, if not eager, to clear himself.

Some of the malice toward Billy drained from the farmer's face, but Robert could tell that there was still suspicion beneath the surface. The preacher and farmer talked intermittently for fifteen minutes as the rolling Missouri countryside crept by. Robert had to puzzle over some of the man's words for a bit while he figured them out. Billy Barnes just closed his eyes and listened.

"No gates left open?" Robert asked. Gunther shook his head.

"Fences down?" They pulled up in front of the house, and Preacher looked about.

"I don't think so. I haven't walked the fence line for a while, though," Gunther said.

"Well, sir, what say we check out the pasture first?" Robert stood in the box to view the visible pasture to the side of the wagon. The topography rose toward the west before it flattened out again, and a large portion of the landscape was not visible past the barn.

To the right, there were several outbuildings. A few hens pecked outside a fenced-in chicken house. "Did you ever find out what happened to your sow?" Robert looked at Gunther.

"Ja, the damn thing crawled under that old building over there, got stuck, and smothered itself. I didn't find it until the smell got bad."

"Ah," Preacher smiled. "So, we know the missing horse is not more orneriness from someone who had it in for you." He glanced at Billy. There was some resistance to the recent German influx of settlers around Pumpkin. There was a lot of fussing about their accents and ways of doing things.

"Ja, I guess that's so," Gunther said.

"Damn, the horse is probably out in that pasture somewhere," Billy swept his hand toward the rolling terrain.

"Maybe. Let's head out and see what we find," Robert started off at a rapid pace. The other two men followed.

Gunther's land comprised an eighty-acre rectangle with the long side fronting along the county road running east and west. The old house, barn, and sheds that Gunther bought with the land were situated up a short lane, on the west forty acres. There was a creek fringed with willows and undergrowth crossing the northeast quarter at an angle. The German had purchased a few dairy cattle that had easy access to the water. He said that he kept them in the newly repaired barn at night. Robert started up the incline following one of the trails the cows had worn across the landscape moving to and from the barn.

The men set out at a good pace past the outbuildings and moved higher to a place where they could see the upper branches of the tree-line just visible beyond the top of the hill. Rabbits bounded away from time to time as they moved through the shin-high grass. They were panting when they reached the high point, and the back of the acreage came into view. Billy was the first to spot the mare.

"Look, over there!" Billy pointed to their left to the property's back corner, where a right-angle stacked-wood fence property line marker formed a junction. A small chestnut mare stood with its head thrust atop the intersecting timbers. A few feet away, a timber wolf limped back and forth on three legs. He lunged at the mare and backed away as she sent her back legs flying.

The men hurried forward. They could see that the mare had gotten in her licks, but some blood and minor bite marks were on her hind legs and quarters as well. The wolf now paced back and forth just out of range of the mare's back hooves. Having failed with his earlier attempts, he appeared to be playing with her, conserving his energy while exhausting her with half-hearted charges. It was working.

The small mare's head was drooping. She kicked again and staggered under her own weight. While they watched, the wolf approached again. The mare launched a one-legged kick that caught nothing but air. The wolf, relentlessly, kept moving.

"Time's running out!" Robert hurried forward, instinctively patting his hip, wishing he was armed. Billy was the only man packing a weapon. The big man pulled his Colt, and they moved silently toward the pair. The mare was exhausted. Each time the wolf attacked, her response was delayed a bit more than before. It was clear that the wolf needed only one chance at the mare's belly to finish her off, and he moved forward to take advantage.

Billy needed a clear shot that did not endanger the mare. He ran hard right, trying to get the angle he needed, but the wolf pacing side to side gave him only seconds to act. The wolf rushed in again, its fangs exposed. Foam dripped from its jaws. The mare gave a feeble response and almost went to her knees. The men knew that she had only seconds to live.

Robert fought the impulse to look away. The men were close now. They could see her chest heaving, her eyes big with fear, and her trembling legs.

Billy was now in range. Robert wondered if the man was any good with the six-gun. If he missed, the wolf would run. He'd be free to stalk the mare on another day. But that wasn't as important right now as saving the mare! Robert wondered if Billy even had time for that one shot before the predator's fangs found the mare's soft belly. It was time! The wolf's narrowed eyes and renewed energy showed that he thought this was his final charge. The mare could not even mount another kick. Instead, she stumbled.

The wolf's rush was around the left side, perhaps thinking of moving along parallel with the stacked rails and reaching the mare's belly.

It was the in-line travel that Billy needed. He sighted down his six-gun with both hands and pulled the trigger. The gun barked once, there was a high-pitched yelp, and as a cloud of gray smoke rose heavenward, the wolf pitched to the side. The mare pressed against the timbers for a moment and then used her last ounce of energy to turn about and rear up again. Without hesitation, she came down with both front hooves on the lifeless body. She stood over her tormentor, heaving from the exertion.

Gunther approached and ran his hand across her flank and her shoulder. He spoke to her gently as he stroked and patted her neck. The mare nickered and tossed its head weakly. He pulled a halter from his back pocket and slipped it over the animal's head.

"Looks like this little girl fought off the wolf for a long time before we got here," Billy said. Robert nodded as he noted the trodden arc of broken ground from her hooves.

"I'll bet he chased her out here and got her backed into this corner thinking he was winning. She probably caught him with her first kick. If she hadn't, she'd of been a goner before we got here. That injured leg smartened him up," Robert said.

"I've heard of horses fighting off wolves, but it don't usually turn out this way," Billy said. Robert studied the carcass. "I bet he's an outcast from a pack. Look, he's old and scarred up. A pack would have run her down in a minute."

"Ja!" The German pulled the mare close and murmured to her. "You are a fine little girl!" He looked at Robert and Billy. "Thank you both." He walked over to Billy and stuck out his hand. "I was wrong. I am sorry I was suspicious of you."

"I told you I didn't do nothing." Billy lifted his head, embarrassed at the attention.

Robert nodded. "Billy, you were a good man to have out here today. I was praying you were a good shot. You proved yourself." He stuck out his hand. Billy hesitated and then shook.

"I guess that goes both ways," Billy said.

"Yep." Robert's big head nodded,

THE END

Sarah,
BLACKBERRIES

"The blackberries are ripe!" Fourteen-year-old Luke Tyson called out as he closed the back door and entered. He dropped a handful on the countertop in the Lucky Star's kitchen. Luke was an athletic-looking boy of medium size. He had dark hair that reached his collar. His green eyes sparkled as he made his announcement, for Luke had a sweet tooth. He was always on the lookout for something sweet. The most readily available fruits in northwest Georgia in spring and early summer were peaches and various berries. The blueberry and strawberry seasons were already over. After filling himself up, Luke had started home with two handfuls of big juicy blackberries. But not able to help himself, he had eaten one handful on the way. Sarah reached over and picked one up and blew on it to remove a shred of a leaf. She popped the thumb-sized berry into her mouth.

Luke was an adventurous young man. He loved roaming the woods and meadows, looking for interesting critters. He was known to jump on a loose horse and ride bareback across the fields on occasion. He was a good runner as well. Though two years younger, Sarah fancied herself able to keep up with him when she chose to. He was her mentor and guide when they weren't fussing with one another. But when Luke wasn't looking for adventure, nothing interested him like reading a book about faraway places. He vowed that someday he'd see the whole world.

"I love blackberries!" Sarah said. Blackberry picking was an annual amusement for the folks in Harlon County. The big purple berries could be found along many roads and on the upper banks of the several creeks that wandered through the valley. An energetic youngster could pick their fill in only a few minutes.

"You children, wait until it's cooler before you go spend a lot of time out there in the sun," Aunt Emmy said. She reached over and picked up two large berries to hand out to the cook and her helper, plus one for herself. It was June 10th, 1857. Temperatures were already in the nineties in the middle of the day. "I'll get out some buckets. Don't forget your high-topped boots. I don't want you-all getting snake bit."

"I hate those boots," Luke complained to Sarah. "Hot and heavy. I bet they're too small since last year." Sarah and Luke had lost their parents to malaria four years before. Their Aunt, Miss Emmy Lawson, had taken them in. The children had arrived just as she was preparing to open the Lucky Star Tavern and Hotel. Before they knew it, they were involved with its daily operation.

"Let's hurry and finish our chores here," Sarah said. The single blackberry had only made her hungry for more. Luke nodded and headed for the back alley to split some recently delivered cordwood into a size useable in the stove. Sarah started clearing and wiping down the last table.

An hour later, the two children were out the door with a two-gallon bucket each. They would be making several excursions over the next few days as their Aunt Emmy would convert most of the berries they picked into jelly. A walk down the road would take them through an area alive with blackberry vines, but they could see that dust from passing wagons covered the berries near the road. So instead, they headed off across the field toward Sandy Creek. The intermittent stream slowed to a trickle in August during the dry season. At the moment, after two months of rain, it was flowing steadily, and the depth varied greatly along its length.

It was there that they ran across Jimmy Jordon. They saw his horse first, reins looped around the branch of a willow tree.

"I recognize that horse," Luke said.

Jimmy stuck his head out of the thicket of blackberry vines just then. "Howdy, Luke!" He nodded shyly toward Sarah. He had half a hatful of blackberries he had collected. He popped one into his mouth. He eyed their buckets. "I guess you're here for berries too. I was riding out on the road and decided to water my horse up yonder." He motioned to a place nearby where a small bridge crossed the creek. "Next thing I knew, I was picking berries." He grinned.

Jimmy was the same age as Luke. They had known each other from before their first school days. They all attended the Baptist church.

Luke looked down the shady bank toward the stream. "I see some huge berries down in that hollow. These boots are killing my feet. I'm going to go down a fill my pail in a hurry so I can take them off."

Sarah nodded and watched as Jimmy disappeared into the brambles again. She moved along the fringe of vines. It seemed silly to fight the brush and berry briers when you could just walk along and pick the outlying berries so easily.

She watched the two boys depart. Jimmy was a little taller than Luke. He lived on a farm a few miles from town. Jimmy was a quiet boy unless he was running with his friends. Sarah imagined that he was busy refilling his hat. Then she heard a surprised cry from the direction of the creek. There was the sound of something tumbling down the bank, followed by some splashing and thrashing around. Then it was silent for a moment before she heard the sound of Luke laughing. Then the laughter was cut short by his swearing.

"Luke! Are you alright?" Sarah moved deeper into the brambles that she had decided only a moment before to avoid. "Luke!!" There was no answer for a moment, and then she heard Luke again.

"Damn, boots are stuck!" Finally, Sarah reached a vantage point where she could see the top of Luke's head. "My feet slipped out from under me. Now I'm buried in these boots halfway to my knees."

"Well, get out of there!"

"I think I'm in quicksand," Luke said as if thinking out loud.

"Quicksand?" Sarah knew that Sandy Creek got its name precisely because of the sandy bottom.

At that moment, Jimmy approached from behind her. "I heard Luke shout?"

"He says he's buried in quicksand."

"Hey, Sarah, Jimmy?" Luke's voice sounded pitched higher than usual. "I'm still sinking! The sand is up to my knees!" His voice trailed off for a moment, then, "Help!"

Sarah had been edging around the worst of the brambles trying to catch a better look at her brother. "I see you, Luke!" What Sarah saw was Luke struggling to stay upright with water now up past his waist. While she watched, the ebb of murky water was inching up further by the minute. Finally, she called back to Jimmy. "Luke is sinking in sand, something terrible." She cast her eyes around, trying to think of a solution. Jimmy hurried to her side.

"Wow, he is sinking fast." Like Sarah, Jimmy's eyes were large with concern. "Wait, I've got a rope!" Sarah heard him crashing back up the bank through the brambles. There was a moment's silence. When he returned, Jimmy had his coiled rope in hand. Without a moment's hesitation, he careened further down the steep bank. "I'm coming, Luke!" Jimmy quickly worked himself down closer to the edge of the water.

"Luke, grab hold!" He called out to his friend. Jimmy readied the rope to toss toward Luke.

By now, the water was up to Luke's chest. He was still straining to get a foot free, so he could grab hold of something, anything to keep from sinking. But the boots were stuck now. Sarah imagined that the loose sand was pouring in the tops by now, making them even heavier. Despite his best efforts, the moving water rippled against Luke's collarbone. His sinking had slowed some, but it hadn't stopped. Jimmy pitched the rope toward Luke, but it snagged and fell short. Sarah could also see how perilously close they were to running out of time. Jimmy leaped the last few feet to the water's edge. He retrieved the rope and threw it again. This time it landed across Luke's shoulder, but both Jimmie and Sarah could see that time was running out.

"Tie it around you under your arms," Jimmy yelled. "Hurry!"

Sarah watched, frozen in place for a moment. Then she realized that Jimmy would not be able to pull Luke out by himself. She threw down her bucket and grabbed the trunk of a willow tree. Sarah allowed herself to slide down the bank toward Jimmy.

"I'm coming, Luke!" She cried out from the pain as the brambles snagged at her legs and arms. She grabbed another willow just below her and slid the rest of the way to stand beside Jimmy.

"He won't be able to pull himself out," Jimmy said. "We'll have to do it!"

Sarah looked toward Luke as the water reached his chin. Jimmy tossed the rope again. Luke caught it but leaning forward caused him to suck in a mouthful of water. He coughed. Jimmy looked back at Sarah. "Hold this!" he tossed her the rope to hold. "We need my horse for this!" Holding the end of the rope, he charged up the eight-foot bank to his waiting horse. The rope strained in Sarah's hands now from both directions. "Can you give me more slack?" Jimmy yelled down at her. She pulled hard, but in doing so, she pulled Luke forward so that his chin was now touching the water. In a sudden panic, Sarah wondered if they would drown Luke trying to save him. Then, she felt the slack jerked out of the rope. It happened so rapidly that Sarah found herself pulled off balance. She looked back at Luke, who sucked a final lungful of air before the water covered his face.

"No!" Sarah cried.

"Quick, pull!" Jimmy yelled down at her. Sarah heard a grunt from above. She wasn't sure if it was Jimmy or the horse. She looked back. The rope was now disappearing into the muddy water. Had they lost him! "Hurry, Jimmy," she called. "Hurry!" The rope moved in her hands. It stretched against Luke's weight an inch and then a foot. Luke's hands came out of the water holding the rope. His head appeared for a moment, and he gasped for breath just as he lost his hold on the line. He disappeared again.

"Luke!" Sarah cried out in renewed panic. "Harder, Jimmy!" Sarah heard Jimmy slap the hindquarter of his horse with the flat of his hand and yelp again.

The rope moved another foot and then two more. Finally, Luke's head reappeared, and he coughed a long-ragged wheeze. His eyes were closed, and his face was twisted with pain.

When Luke could reach the bank, he grabbed a willow and held it close as he rested his cheek against his hands. Sarah called back at Jimmy.

"He's out!" She studied Luke. "Are you okay?" After a moment, he nodded and coughed again.

"He's okay!" Sarah shouted up to Luke.

Jimmy clambered down the bank and helped Luke to his feet. His look of concern changed as Luke came out of the water. His boots and socks were missing. "Do you always go berry picking barefoot?" Jimmy grinned.

Luke flexed his ankle. "Those damn boots almost got me drowned. If I could have gotten my feet out of them, I could have floated out. But instead, the boots kept sinking and pulling me down with them."

Sarah looked at her brother. "I was going to be pretty mad if you drowned," she said. Luke and Jimmy grinned.

"Don't make a little sister mad." Jimmy admonished

"Well, I try not to," Luke replied solemnly. "But it's tough, sometimes!"

Sarah smiled. Luke and Aunt Emmy were all she had in the world. She cast her eyes toward Jimmy. She knew she'd never forget the day the tall, shy boy saved a big piece of her world. She pulled a berry from a bush at eye level. She was glad to have everyone survive to pick berries another day.

THE END

Maggie, UNWELCOME ATTENTION

The true paternity of John Jones' young slave, Brownie, was revealed to Maggie Taylor at the end of a chain of unwelcome events. In truth, she had little awareness of the boy's history or the man who made the revelation. But sometimes, people tell more than others want to know.

Promptly at two o'clock on a sunny Saturday in July, twenty-one-year-old Maggie heard a knock on her front door. Mister Fredrick Ingerstall Junior, forty-nine, stood outside holding a bouquet. Maggie's glance out the window brought first a moment's confusion and then the memory of their conversation the previous week. She had reluctantly invited the man for tea! Her mind raced for a moment over their interaction of July 4th.

Maggie was an attractive young lady when events forced her into the role of an independent woman at an early age. And she was moderately prosperous. However, Maggie discovered that the aura of prosperity proved magnetic to men of all stations. The extent of Maggie Taylor's affluence was unknown to her neighbors, but she owned her own home and dressed modestly and well. Most of the citizens of Titustown in Harlon County, Georgia, were too involved with their own affairs to concern themselves with the finances of the young homebody.

When she was nineteen, Arnold Taylor, Maggie's father, was the last of her parents to pass away. He left her a farm at the end of a country road near Homestead Mountain. Arnold had also acquired modest interests in half a dozen companies via the New York Stock Exchange over the last twenty years of his life through prudent savings and investments. He also owned a small stake in the local bank. It was the banking connection that led to her introduction to the middle-aged Ingerstall.

Upon her father's death, Maggie successfully sold the farm and moved to town. The terms of the sale were to provide her with an annual income at harvest time. Maggie's small house, a block from the Baptist Church, provided convenient access to church activities, important because she had played the piano for the services there since its founding the previous year. Over her young life, there had been few entanglements with the opposite sex beyond friendly social exchanges. She lived a simple and re-spectable life centered on her church.

But then, she had inadvertently come to the attention of Mis-ter Fredrick Ingerstall Junior. Mister Ingerstall had been mar-ried to a girl from Savannah. He had brought her home to live with his parents on one of the best farms in the area. She was a beautiful girl and settled in comfortably. She had even brought her old house slave, Suzy, with her. Unfortunately, Suzy had contracted tuberculosis in the slave quarters of the bride's home in Savannah. Suzy promptly shared her affliction with her mistress and Frederick's mother. By 1840 both Frederick Senior and Fredrick Junior were widowers, and the elder had started a long slow decline.

Following the War of 1812, which many patriots considered the second war for independence, many communities in America sponsored celebrations on July 4th honoring Revolutionary War veterans. After the establishment of a Baptist Church in Titustown, it joined with the Methodist church co-sponsoring a July social to honor veterans of the two conflicts. Preoccupied with unfolding a banner, the two men caught Maggie off guard when they approached.

"Miss Taylor, how are you today?" Mister Elvis Thurman, the bank's Chief Cashier, and a man she knew well appeared at her elbow. "I'd like to introduce a friend of mine." He smiled broadly and glanced toward the other man. "Mister Frederick Ingerstall Junior and his father are depositors at the bank," he explained.

Maggie's eyes flitted from the younger man's face into the eyes of the older Fred Ingerstall Junior. He was much taller than she, with lean facial features and a receding hairline. He had pleasant gray eyes, a prominent mustache, and thick eyebrows. His nose was short with wide flaring nostrils. His lips stretched over uneven teeth when he smiled.

"Very nice to meet you, sir." Maggie gave him her pleasant but somewhat non-committal smile. Harlon County was still sparsely settled, and she was aware of the Ingerstall family. However, since both surviving Ingerstall gentlemen were older, male, and Methodists, they had never been part of her social circle. Nevertheless, Maggie's recollection that the younger Fred had lost both his wife and mother several years before brought a touch of sympathy that brightened her response.

"Very nice to meet you, Miss Taylor!" Fred responded. He glanced at Mister Thurman meaningfully. Then, having complied with Ingerstall's request for the introduction, Elvis found a fascinating conversation about road construction nearby and excused himself.

"There aren't many of the old Revolutionary boys around anymore," Fred mused.

"True, but we still have a dozen 1812 men in the county. One old fellow rode over from Clarksville to get recognized," Maggie grinned.

Fred Junior's face registered indifference at her little joke. "My father participated briefly in that conflict. I think he was disappointed that it ended so abruptly. I remember his buying a new uniform and disappearing for six months. Then, he moped about the farm for another six months after he returned."

"I wasn't born yet." Maggie tried again at some fun. The comment about "moped" had sparked some hope that a secret sense of humor lurked in the man's breast, but again her effort fell flat. The middle-aged man's features remained immobile.

"Well, I need to go make some more preparations, Mister Ingerstall." She held out her hand, pleased at an opportunity to depart gracefully.

A surprised look lighted the older man's eyes for a moment, then he took her hand and bowed rather formally, she thought, for strangers parting at a picnic.

"May I call on you, Miss Taylor?" The man's expression was unexpectedly earnest.

Maggie stared at him, a bit confused. She could not imagine the cause of his interest. She estimated that he was at least twice her age. Then Maggie realized that her age was possibly only one of several reasons for his interest. Her intuition instructed her to decline, but she remembered the deceased wife again, and her natural sympathy and good manners won out.

"I suppose." She was surprised that she could not come up with a polite refusal. Everything that came to mind sounded blunt and even harsh. "Why yes, that might be nice." Maggie recovered her southern manners quickly. "I should be happy to have you for tea next Saturday at two." She raised her eyebrows and watched his mind grasp both the invitation and the fact that it was for a time and date a whole week away.

"Perfectly fine," he replied after a moment. "So, I will call at two o'clock?"

Maggie nodded, bid Fred goodbye, and went into the church to make more preparations. The encounter left hardly a trace across her consciousness until the man's knock rattled her front door a week later, and she looked out and saw the flowers.

"Mister Ingerstall!" Maggie opened the door and accepted the flowers with an appreciative "ahh!" She stepped back. "Please be seated here on my side porch where it is shady." The man followed her through the parlor to a small east-facing porch. "If you will excuse me for a moment, I'm afraid I lost track of time. I'll put the kettle on the stove for tea."

Maggie delayed her departure long enough to catch the look of consternation pass across Fred's features before he nodded. He passed through the outer door to sit in one of two green ladder-back chairs separated by a small white table. A breeze moved the surrounding bushes and fluttered the overhang of the crocheted table cloth.

Maggie always did her week's baking on Saturday. Fortunately, the stove was already hot from the cookies she had just taken out of the oven. Maggie smiled to herself. The scent of her baking filled the house and was a convenient cover for her total amnesia regarding the prearranged tea. Mister Ingerstall could assume if he wished that she baked the cookies, especially for their get-together. She thrust the flowers into a vase half-filled with water and joined the man on the porch. Maggie's primary interest centered on sending the man on his way as soon as socially acceptable.

"So, how are you today, Sir? I'm afraid we are going to have a typical Georgia July."

"Yes, I agree. We can be thankful for the breeze." Mister Ingerstall studied Maggie in silence for a long moment. She was quite pleasant looking. Her eyebrows arched in a particularly exotic way. The brown eyes were alert, the teeth good.

Maggie noticed the evaluation and immediately compared the process with a domestic animal for sale on the block. Didn't men study a horse to be purchased in the same way? She purposefully bared her teeth in a little private joke and listened attentively for the sound of the teapot.

"So, what is the purpose of your visit, sir?" Even at a young age, Maggie felt the need to sort things out and clarify the objectives and motivations of the people with whom she interacted.

"Well, Miss Taylor, I couldn't help notice you at the social. I find you very attractive. I inquired with Elvis Thurman about you, and he mentioned that you have an interest in the bank." He paused as if the rest was self-explanatory.

Maggie's exotic eyebrows rose artfully. "How does that interest you, sir?"

Fred found the young lady's directness both unusual and disquieting. "I understand that your father was a man of many interests in addition to his shares in the bank?" Fred stirred in his chair just as the whistling teapot interrupted them.

The man's uncommon interest in her finances raised Maggie's ire. She leaped to her feet and let the screen door slam as she retired to the kitchen. Maggie returned with the tea, cups, saucers, and a bowl of cookies arranged on a silver tray. She could tell by the older man's expression that he read a lot into small gestures such as cookies with the tea. He watched appreciatively while she expertly poured the tea and offered him a cookie.

"We have an excellent cook at our farm, but I'm sure that her cookies don't surpass these," he said after taking a second bite. Fred gave her a congratulating smile. Maggie noted the small boast concerning servants and the assumption regarding the cookies. However, she remained miffed at his interest in her finances. Maggie decided a balloon deserved popping.

"Luckily, Saturday is my regular baking day." Maggie took a small nibble. It was delicious. Maggie didn't know what to make of the interest the man was exhibiting toward her. It was disquieting if she was honest with herself. But there seemed to be no alternative but to carry on. After an hour's aimless chitchat, none of which provided any clear indication of the man's motivations, they parted. The repeat of the formal farewell offered after the social seemed more appropriate after an hour's interaction, but not much.

The following morning Maggie arrived early at the church to review the hymns for the Sunday service. She was surprised to find Fred Ingerstall out front conversing with the Baptist Minister, Reverend Hopkins. The men smiled as she approached.

The old preacher smiled knowingly. "You seem to have a positive effect on our Methodist brethren."

"I do?"

"Yes, Mister Ingerstall tells me he may join our church."

Maggie's head swung toward Fred Junior. "Not on my account, I hope."

Fred smiled tightly. "I'm told you are very involved in the church and that you play the piano wonderfully. And I've heard that Pastor Hopkins is a good preacher. All good reasons to give his church a try."

Reverend Hopkins smiled, shook Fred's hand, and excused himself to do a last review of the morning's sermon. At that moment, a young black boy ran past accompanied by a white boy of approximately the same age. Maggie knew them to be twelve or thirteen. Both boys had reached the age when their boyish features had begun to flatten out into the planes and hollows of young men in the making. She knew both well. Madison Jones was seldom unaccompanied by his father's young slave, Brownie. Maggie noticed that for some reason, Fred turned his face away and stroked his jaw.

The boys were an unusual pair. There was no master and servant attitude between them as they chased about playing tag with other children before the service. But then, the morning light caught the boy's face just right, and she startled a little. There was a strange similarity between the boy's features and those of the middle-aged man standing before her. Fred Junior's swift motion to turn away did more toward fixing her recognition than easing it. The boys ran away and then zig-zagged back toward them. Brownie passed again behind Fred just as he moved his hand from his jaw down to his coat pocket. There was a striking resemblance between the black boy and Fred Ingerstall Junior! No, not just some resemblance; a clear likeness!

When Fred realized that the boys had returned, he again attempted to cover his features, but it was too late, and he knew it. His eyes glanced guiltily toward Maggie. Before he could speak, she sought to end the conversation.

"Well, I have hymns to look over." Maggie hurried up the steps and entered the vestibule. Once seated at the piano, she flipped through pages of the hymnal using the preacher's list of selections that he had left on the music rack for her.

She found the first hymn and started on *Bringing in the Sheaves.* She had just run through the song, and was turning to the second when she heard the front door open. A glance told her that Fred Ingerstall was approaching.

"You saw it, didn't you." Fred didn't mince words.

"Yes," Maggie answered. "That little boy, Brownie, is your son, isn't he?"

"No!" Fred sat down heavily on the front pew. "It's just as bad, though. He's my brother or at least half brother."

"Ahh, your father." Maggie let her hands fall to her lap.

"He was only eight when my father sold him to Jack Jones five years ago. You can see as well as I that the older he gets, the more our common features give it away."

"So, why are you telling me this?" Maggie crossed her arms.

"Because I don't want this to come between us since we're courting."

"Between us?" Maggie blanched. "Mister Ingerstall, I have no interest in the resemblance between you and Brownie, the nature of your relationship, or any of the rest of it. And we are not courting! I'm sure you are a fine man and a good southern gentleman and all that. But, of course, you have no responsibility for your father's procreation habits. May I repeat myself? We are not now, nor will we ever be courting! You are twice my age!" She leaned her head back and looked at the lofty ceiling for a moment. "Again, sir, we are not courting."

"You're only five years younger than my late wife when she died."

"Well, your late wife died several years ago. So I'm suitable as a friend but not as a companion in any other sense!"

"But we have so much in common."

"Well, yes," she replied with a touch of sarcasm, "We both enjoy tea and cookies. We both enjoy piano music. That's all we know about each other, isn't it."

"That doesn't mean we aren't suitable," Fred said defensively.

Maggie's patience had run out.

"Mister Ingerstall, you are not invited for tea and cookies ever again. If you wish to lengthen the time until the whole town recognizes your shared parentage with that little black boy outside, you will confine your worship to the Methodist Church down the road. There, direct comparisons will not be so readily available. If you insist on attending this church on Sunday, please do not sit closer than five rows from my piano." Maggie closed the hymnal decisively. "I hope I make myself clear. Excuse me, please. I have other errands to take care of before the service begins." Just then, the first parishioners entered, ensuring an end to the conversation.

Fred made a face. "You won't say anything about Brownie and me, will you?" He was almost whispering now.

"Of course not." Maggie drew back at the suggestion. "If anyone ever knows anything about it, it will be because they managed to figure it out for themselves or were told by someone other than myself." She rose and stepped around the bench. "I wish you the best, Sir. Good day." With that, Maggie Taylor walked toward the door to greet one of her friends. She had the nagging feeling that trouble followed Mister Fredrick Ingerstall Junior. He seemed entirely too eager to stray into unknown territory.

THE END

Bronco, WILLOW

Bill looked out over the lot with Edgar and the farm's owner, Mister Sam Jacobs. In one field, horses that Bill had already broken grazed together. The horses yet to be ridden were in the pasture next door. It seemed like any other day until Sam felt the first pains in his chest. He clasped his hands over his heart and half doubled over for a moment. But after few quick breaths, the older man claimed he was fine. Bill and Edgar wanted to hitch up the wagon to get him to the doctor. Instead, he sent them on to get started with the day's work. But at supper, Sam went to bed early. That left the men with a subject that neither wanted to talk about. They avoided each other's eyes, and it was unnaturally quiet for a while before they turned in. They rose the next morning, hoping the hail and hardy Sam would show up for breakfast like always, but Sam didn't show up at all. Edgar went back to Sam's room and got orders, and the two men went to work as usual. Bill had hay to stack, and Edgar went for a ride on one of the newly broken horses. When he returned, he was giving the animal a few unpleasant words.

"Dang!" Edgar said. "Bronco, you may have to break this big bay again. He reared up half a dozen times. My bones are getting too brittle for this line of work." Bill Brumley watched Edgar stumble after dismounting from the bay stallion. Then the older man limped over toward one of the three old ladderback chairs the boss had lined up against the side of the barn. Edgar sat and crossed his arms to massage out the soreness in his biceps. Then, finally, he looked across the corral and heaved a sigh. Sam Jacobs' farm in southeast Ohio had received a shipment of between fifty and a hundred wild mustangs every three or four months since the war started. Sam, Edgar, and Bill took turns breaking the horses when the young Bill Brumley first arrived, but Sam had gotten too old to climb on a horse anymore, and Edgar came close to breaking some part of himself every time one of the half-broke horses threw him.

Almost two years had passed since Bill showed up at Sam's door looking for work after his grandfather passed away. He had grabbed the job Sam offered before he knew what the duties would be. Bill was a small-town boy without horse riding experience, but he was game to try. It quickly became apparent that Bill was limber enough, strong enough, and possessed sufficient sense of balance to be a natural bronc-buster. Bill knew that Edgar, whose age was somewhere over fifty, was several years younger than Sam Jacobs, the farm's owner. Jacobs had begun to use the Bronco nickname for Bill shortly after his arrival. The boss seemed to sense from the beginning that the young man had potential. Bill had felt that Edgar was skeptical initially, but when Bill outlasted every bronc he slung his leg across, he convinced Edgar as well. After a while, Edgar joined the older man in calling him Bronco.

Soon, Bill had the job of taking the first hard-bucking ride of each of the green horses. The two older men rode them after they bucked themselves out to gentle them down some more. The demand for more horses came alongside the growing casualties of Union soldiers and their horses as the war between north and south progressed. The death and injury count for the animals was higher than for the men, and supply had never caught up with demand.

Edgar sat down heavily, leaned the chair back against the side of the barn, and closed his tired eyes for a moment. He rubbed the back of his hand against his grizzled jaw and spoke again as Bill approached. "Bronco, Sam says he got word that the fella from the army will be here in three days. I counted eight horses yet to break. How are you holding up?"

Bill was tall, trim, and well-muscled. His brown curly hair covered his ears but was short of his shoulders. He dusted off his pants and pulled off his gloves as he sat down in the adjacent chair. By coincidence, Bill would be twenty years old in three days.

"They ain't getting any easier, are they?" He grinned, and Edgar noted that his voice had picked up some resonance over the last months. Then Bill's smile faded.

"How is Mister Sam feeling? He seemed pretty puny yesterday even after he said he was alright." Early on, Bill had taken to sleeping in the barn on warm nights. He loved being with the horses and preferred the hay to his regular bed. He rubbed his well-callused hands together. They were rough despite the protection the gloves provided.

"I don't know," Edgar said. "Sam told me this morning that he gets a sharp pain in his chest from time to time. Says he feels weak."

Bill frowned. "My grandpa had that sometimes. But he was some older than Mister Sam." He brightened. "And don't forget he always perks up some when the buyer comes around and he gets paid."

"That's true." Edgar nodded, but he seemed skeptical that a fistful of money could help his friend this time.

"Am I going to the store today, or are you?" Bill leaned forward as if to stand.

"You go Bronco. I'm tuckered already, " Edgar said. "Get some money out of the jar. Sam made a list. It's on the table."

Bill entered the house and found that Sam was still abed. He stuck his head in the door. "Mister Sam, Mister Edgar said I was to go into town. Is everything you want on the list?"

Sam Jacobs was lying in bed with his head turned toward the wall. He looked around and managed to smile at the younger man, but he seemed distracted.

"Yeah. Did Edgar tell you the buyer is coming in the next few days?"

"Yes, sir. I'm going to jump on a couple more horses when I get back from town."

"That's good, Bronco." Sam seemed to be short of breath. He reached up and lay his hand on Bronco's forearm for a moment. It was one of several signs of affection the old man exhibited with his friends. Placing his hand on a shoulder, a swat on the back or a tousle of Bill's hair said what the old man didn't know how to verbalize.

"Sir, maybe we should hitch up the wagon and take you in to see the doc?" Bill felt a chill run up his spine. Sam seemed much weaker than he had been the previous day. Bronco noticed how his arm dropped back to his chest.

"The truth is, I don't feel up to the trip," Sam admitted. "Why don't you stop in and ask Doc Riles if he can give you something to bring to me?"

"Yes, sir." Bronco grabbed the list and, finding the bay still saddled, climbed aboard. The big horse gathered himself to rear up. Bronco settled him down and rode over to Edgar.

"Mister Sam wants me to stop in the doc's and see if he has anything that could help him. He's still in bed."

"Good. But it would be a better idea though if the doctor came out hisself."

"I'll try that."

The bay reared again. Bill kicked it and rode hard out the gate. After a half-mile running full out, the horse slowed. Bill spurred it back into a full-out gallop. It was good for another quarter and then slowed again.

"We ain't got time to fool around," Bill said. "Remember when you were so full of vim and vigor this morning with Edgar?" He gave the horse a bit of a breather; then, they took off again.

Upon reaching the doctor's office, Bill read the note on the door saying that the doctor would be back shortly. Bill used the delay to ride down the block and enter the general store to pick up the things on his list. The doctor was in when he returned to the office. He found the man sitting at a desk.

"Sir, my name is Bill Brumley. I work for Mister Sam Jacobs. I'm real worried about him, sir. He says he has pains in his chest and didn't want to even get out of bed to come to see you!"

Doctor Riles eyed the young man. He could see that Bill was alarmed. "Sounds like he has heart trouble." He grimaced. "I'd go out right now, but I'm on my way out to deliver a baby." He looked at a shelf full of bottles and jars that Bill deduced were medical concoctions. "Looks like I'm out of anything that might help him." He seemed to think for a minute. "When you get home, go out and pick a big batch of willow leaves. Cut them up into small pieces and boil them for about an hour to make a tea. When it cools down, give Sam about half a cup to drink. It might help, or it might not."

"Yes, sir!" Bill left the office and leaped on the bay.

Bill rode hard, feeling that somehow, he was racing against time. He didn't see either of the men when he rode up. Rather than look for Edgar, he went straight to the barn, where he knew he could find a bushel basket. The closest approach to the creek was where it ran parallel to the road. Basket in hand, Bill mounted the bay again and rode down the side ditch into a stand of willow trees. Then, he thought he smelled smoke.

"What's the basket for?" A man was sitting alone under a large willow tree. The cascading branches reached the ground and obscured him from sight. If Bill had not detected the smoke or horse tied nearby, he might have missed him altogether had he not spoken.

Bill dismounted and parted the streamers of willow branches to address the man. As Bill approached, the man leaned forward to breathe in the steam from a pan of water. He was dressed in a loose deerskin jacket and wore a round beaver head-covering with two feathers attached to the right side. A beaded necklace with a leather pouch hung down on his chest. His rifle leaned against the tree.

"I'm here for willow leaves," Bill said. "My boss has pain in his chest, and the doctor said to collect some willow leaves and cook them up for him."

"Willow is good medicine," the man said. He stuck out his hand. "I am Piqua. I am a Shawnee."

"Glad to meet you, sir. I need to start collecting those leaves right now. Mister Sam was in a bad way when I left him!" Bill set down the basket and started stripping the leaves from the nearby hanging branches. He could have a basket full in no time.

Piqua held up his hand. "I do not know why it is so, but my people have discovered that the most valuable part of the willow is the joint where the leaf detaches from the branch. He pointed at the end of a stem where a tiny bulb-like protrusion connected the branch and the stem. "Good medicine is strongest there. So when you pull the leaf away, be sure to take that with it. Then lay the leaves side by side like this." Piqua lay several leaves and stems parallel to each other, and using his knife, sliced off the stems just above the bulb.

"When you have enough to fill the palm of your hand, heat them in twice as much water until it starts to boil. When it cools, let your friend drink the broth. It will make his stomach hurt a little. So he should not drink too much or take it more than twice a day for three days."

Bill listened intently. He did not know this man, and he had seen very few Indians before. Bill knew that most had left Ohio many years back, but the man was old, spoke with authority, and took the time to explain things to him while the doctor had been hurried and explained little. So, Bronco changed his method of harvesting leaves to ensure that he took the bulb when he shucked the leaves off of the stems. Then, when the basket was full, he turned to the man.

"Thank you, sir. I have a feeling that Mister Sam may not have a lot of time left for him, but maybe these leaves will buy him a little more." He leaned down to shake the Indian's hand. Then, he mounted the bay, spurred the horse from the creek to the road, and hightailed it back to the farm.

Edgar was standing on the porch when Bill rode up. He stepped off and approached Bill as he dismounted.

"Where'd you go? I saw you out the window. What's in the basket?"

Bill had piled the groceries in the basket with the leaves to make it easier to carry everything. He headed toward the house with it as he related his experiences with the doctor in town and the Indian, Piqua, in the willow stand.

"I ain't trusting no Indian, but since the doc told you the same thing, I guess we should do it," Edgar opined.

The two men entered the kitchen, and Bronco showed Edgar how to organize the leaves to slice off the tiny bulbs from the stems. Bill estimated that a palm-full of bulbs equaled half a cup, so he dropped them into the heating water when he had a cup full. As soon as the water started to boil, he set it off the fire to cool.

Bill went back into the bedroom to report to Sam. The older man was clutching his chest and panting.

"This is a bad one, Bronco." He tapped his chest with his fingers. "It comes and goes. Did the doc come back with you?"

"No, sir, but he told me about some medicine I could make that might help. So Mister Edgar and I have been making it up since I got home." They heard the sound of footsteps in the hall. Edgar came in with a cup of steaming broth and a jar of honey.

"I done tasted this here brew, and it's a might bitter. You might like to have some honey mixed in?"

Sam raised his hand and accepted the cup. He breathed in the fumes and sipped a bit. "Argh!" He made a face. "This won't ever replace coffee or tea. Pour in a goodly amount of honey, Edgar!"

Edgar took the cup back, set it on the dresser, and added a couple of spoonfuls of honey. He stirred it, handed it back, and without a word or a sip, Sam clutched his chest with one hand and threw the concoction back as if it were a shot of whiskey.

"Best to take medicine quick. But the honey at least leaves a pleasant taste in the mouth afterward." He lowered his head to the pillow. There was sweat on his forehead. "It makes an impression when it hits your stomach, too! But, thanks for the trouble, boys. If it's all the same to you, I'd like to be alone for a while. It's feeling right close in here." He gave the men a wane smile, then tucked both hands to his chest before closing his eyes.

Edgar and Bill eyed each other for a minute. Then, finally, they left the room, and Edgar started cleaning up the mess of discarded leaves in the kitchen. Bronco had promised to break a couple of broncs, so he went out and unsaddled the bay and released it in the pasture of broken horses. By the time Bill had lassoed another wild horse, Edgar had come out of the house. He was standing by the gate. Bill noticed streaks on his cheeks.

"What's the matter, Mister Edgar?" Bill felt like the pit of his stomach had dropped out.

"Sam passed a couple a minutes ago," Edgar said. The older man propped his elbow up on the gate. "He called me in, and he was telling me that he was feeling some better, and then he grabbed his chest and was gone."

Bill felt the tears swell in his eyes. "But we gave him the broth!"

"Well, yeah, but you said the doc told you it might help or it might not."

Bronco shielded his eyes with his forearm for a second to hide the tears. He remembered the deaths in his life. His mother, grandmother, and grandfather were all gone. He wondered momentarily if his Pa was still alive. He might never know the answer to that question. Now Mister Sam was gone.

"Bronco, Sam said he wanted to be sure we had all the horses ready for the army when the man comes. So reckon you could go ahead a break a couple more today?"

Edgar nodded toward the grove of trees west of the house. "Mrs. Jacobs is buried out there, and I reckon Sam will be too. I'm tired, but I'll ride into town and let the preacher know we're about to have a funeral tomorrow."

Bill nodded. He felt a new wave of sorrow at the thought of the burying. He wiped his eyes with the back of his hand. "Yes, sir." He set his jaw as he always did when he had an unpleasant chore to do. But this time, it wasn't the chore that unsettled him. Sam had given Edgar and Bill so much that the thought of it made his throat raw. The men got the blanket and saddle on one of the wild horses. Then Bill remembered something that consoled him a little. Mister Sam had said that Bill's brew mixed with honey left a good taste in his mouth. That was something. Looking back, it seemed like the only good thing about that day.

THE END

Preacher, A WORTHY CALLING

Pumpkin, Missouri. The Reverend Robert Gracey was a stout, well-muscled man with a prominent jaw and a gap between his upper front teeth. He spoke with a booming voice that could shake the rafters if he let it. But his sermons typically aimed at educating or convincing his congregation rather than frightening them with damnation.

Then Robert lost his church so suddenly that the memory of it still unsettled him days later. When he was upset, Robert calmed himself by walking and prayer, so the man the whole town called Preacher or Brother Gracey strolled along Pumpkin's Main Street while he pondered the chain of events that had gotten him into trouble with his deacons.

Things started going haywire the Sunday Robert preached a sermon posing an alternative viewpoint to the doctrine of free will. What if the omniscient, all-powerful God didn't just monitor His human creations but controlled all of their thoughts and acts? What if that moment-to-moment intervention determined their destiny rather than their own choices?

That question came to the forefront as Robert noted a scripture that he had read without pause in the past. He was rereading the Old Testament book of Exodus concerning the Israelite's efforts to escape enslavement in Egypt, and one verse struck him. The scriptures explained that God sent several horrible plagues and pestilences against the Egyptians in an alleged effort to convince the Pharaoh to release the Israelites from captivity. But just as the Pharaoh 'decided' to release them, "*God hardened his heart*" Exodus 9:12, and the ruler again denied Moses their freedom. This interference seemed at cross purposes to Robert. God abused the ruler and the Egyptian people to force a specific decision and then denied the Pharaoh the ability to make it! Wasn't God overruling the man's free will?

Once Robert began to scrutinize the scriptures seeking either correction or confirmation for his interpretation, the more examples he found. Finally, he reached the point where he wondered if the presumption of free will was ever a correct interruption of the scriptures. It did not take many sermons hinting at this line of thought to put Robert at odds with his deacons, and posing the question as a 'what if ' had not assuaged their concerns.

The country was almost two years into the war when Robert lost his church after twenty years of service. Had he become complacent? Was he guilty of heretical thinking, or were the deacons lazy thinkers? Robert wondered if his pro-Union sentiments had anything to do with it. Missouri was a cauldron of conflict between state officials who were southern sympathizers and those citizens who opposed secession from the very outset. There were members on both sides of that divide in his congregation. Most of the German immigrants were pro-Unionists. As the church leader, Robert had sought to be a calming influence between the two factions. In terms of his churchly duties, the onset of the war resulted in a rash of weddings performed before the young men went off, both to save the Union and oppose it.

As the war approached and the armies of the North and the South faced each other, Robert didn't trouble himself with thoughts of joining the conflict, for he was a minister of the gospel and had a flock to shepherd. He tried to cut short any arguments between his parishioners or when he heard some of his neighbors speak with great relish about taking up arms. Yet, he didn't find pacifism tolerable either, as he felt that pacifism led to the suppression of men of goodwill rather than their ascendancy. The common expectation in Missouri was for a short war. Then, when the war dragged on, Robert had funerals to perform. There were a lot of funerals.

Robert worried that he had lost his calling when he lost his church. When his setback occurred, he was glad that his parents had already passed away. They had been proud of him and encouraged his progress as the Baptist Minister mentored him toward fulfilling his calling. He knew that his 'failure' would have been even more painful to them than it was to him.

Robert was thinking of his calling, the mentoring, and twenty years of serving when he ended his walk by sitting on a bench in front of the Huggins Hardware Store. He watched his neighbors going about their business while he pondered his dismissal. It was Saturday. Many of the passersby were members of the Baptist Church, his church until only a few days before.

Thinking about the events of the last few days brought a hymn to Robert's mind, and he leaned forward and hummed to himself. Occasionally he spoke aloud the words to his favorite parts. *"I'll fly away, old glory, I'll fly away."* He yearned to fly away. He felt dejected. He could go to another town, he supposed. Robert believed God was in charge and pretty confident that He wouldn't have him sit on that bench forever! There was a plan for him. God would reveal it when He was ready! But when?

Off on the side street, a company of Union soldiers marched in cadence with a snare drum. A young man in the lead was carrying a sign that read: *Save the Union. Join the 23rd infantry.* Robert watched the Stars and Stripes and the unit flag pass down the street. Robert had never given thought to army service, for he was a peaceable man. Robert did not seek a fight, nor did he flee from one. Instead, he leaned back and worried some, despite himself, about how God would reveal his next assignment.

The hours went by. Mister Huggins, the owner of the hardware store, came out and swept the walk. He greeted Robert, went back in, and in a bit, returned with a glass of water and inquired if Brother Gracey needed anything. Robert thanked him for the water but indicated he was alright. The morning passed into the afternoon.

Eventually, a young Union soldier came along and sat down on the other end of the bench. He was at least twenty years younger than Robert. The older man guessed that a blade did not need to pass often over the peach-fuzzed face.

"I see you're a preacher," the soldier observed.

Robert looked down at himself. He was wearing an ordinary gray suit and tie. The clue to his identity was probably the simple cross on a chain that encircled his collar and hung below the knotted tie. Given the absence of an actual church, Robert wondered if it was a lie to nod in the affirmative but decided he was merely between churches until God said otherwise.

"Yes."

"What denomination?"

"Baptist."

"My cousin is a Methodist."

"Your cousin?"

"Yes, he's a Methodist Preacher." The young man scratched his neck. "Over in Dover."

"I didn't think he was here in Pumpkin." Robert thought the local Methodist pastor was too old to be the young man's cousin.

"No, over in Dover. I'm here today to see my girl."

"Ah."

"My cousin has joined the army too."

"Oh?"

"Yes, he thinks he should do his part."

Robert considered that for a moment. "I wish him well. What is his name?"

The young man nodded and scratched his neck again. "Thompkins, same as mine. I've been in training. I'm on leave. I'll be here through next week."

"Well, I wish you well also," Robert said.

Robert had inherited a farm at the edge of Pumpkin and raised livestock in addition to his church duties. Leaving town for another church was complicated by his ownership of the farm. He had rented out the farrier shop since his father passed away to an older man from Germany. He supposed he could rent the farm out as well.

The young man stiffened. "There are those Mahoney boys from Dover."

"Oh?" Robert followed the young man's gaze. Two rough-looking young men were swinging up the street. They had a Confederate flag that they playfully tossed back and forth between themselves. Since they were coming from the direction of the marching Union troops, Robert surmised that they might have been conducting a counter-show of loyalty.

"They have kin in South Carolina," Tompkins said. "Their family is hard on the side of secession. I've had run-ins with them before."

The young men approached the two men on the bench from Robert's side and were almost upon them before noticing the young man in the Union uniform.

"Whoa!" The men halted. Ignoring Robert, they addressed Thompkins.

"Well, look here. Here's that sissy Union girl all spruced up to go kill some good old southern boys." The oldest boy waved his flag provocatively inches from Thompkins' face.

Thompkins flinched his head away and offered a terse smile. He did not seem to be intimidated so much as annoyed. "Just doing my duty to my country. You boys should consider doing the same," he retorted.

"Just doing my duty to my country." The younger boy's singsong repetition of Thompkins' words stirred something in Robert.

"Well, you better hurry. Lee has just about won the war. Missouri will be officially seceding just any day now," the older Mahoney boy said. "We'd be Confederacy already, except the state is floating in Germans who're Union." He glanced at Robert. "How about you, Mister. You tied in with these Yankees?"

"The Union has Missouri safely in hand, whatever the secessionists may claim. Mr. Thompkins and I met a few minutes ago, but yes, I favor holding the Union together. I have no interest in either owning slaves or permitting others to do so."

"It ain't just slaves, Mister. It's interfering with the South's cotton and rice production and closing the ports. My old man says the North wants to choke the life out of the southern states, and the states have the right to leave the Union if they want to."

Robert glanced at Thompkins, who was alert to the drift of the conversation, and then up at the faces of the two young men. "The 'interfering' you speak of and the 'states rights' you mention is just a hollow backdoor argument to justify the right to subjugate other human beings for profit. So now you boys take your foreign flag and trot on down the street."

The two young men looked at the stocky preacher and the young Union recruit for a moment. Robert could tell they measured their prospects if they turned the heat up a notch.

"Okay, we're going." The oldest boy handed the flag to the younger and snatched the Union cap from Thompkins' head. He grinned and tucked it inside his jacket. "We'll just take this back to the house and burn it." They took off walking briskly.

"Hey!" Thompkins leaped to his feet and started after them.

Robert watched bemused for a moment, but when the boys ran around the corner into an alley with Tompkins close behind, he felt his concern rise. Robert stood and joined the pursuit. He walked rapidly toward the corner as Tompkins appeared to tumble out into the street. The soldier jumped up and disappeared into the alley again.

Robert felt his heart quicken. He arrived just in time to see the boys disappear around the back corner of the dry goods store. Tompkins was standing, breathing hard, his eye already swelling.

"You okay?" Robert asked.

"Yep!" The young man grinned. He gingerly touched his eye. "I got my licks in too." Tompkins stuck out his hands, showing his skinned knuckles." And I've got my cap back!" He dusted off the blue cap against his leg and pulled it down snugly on his head.

"You should report this to the sheriff," Robert said.

"Nah! They're just ignorant country boys." He looked at Robert closely. "You're a pretty good talker, what with putting down states' rights and such. Maybe you should join the army too?"

Robert pursed his lips, and the two men walked back toward the bench. "Has your cousin already left?"

"No, he leaves next week. He's known our Congressman for a long time. He went through him to get his commission to serve as a chaplain." The young man waved at a pretty girl coming out of the Huggins Hardware Store. Robert recognized her as Mister Huggins' daughter and a member of the Baptist Church. That explained why the young man had been sitting out front with him.

"I'm going to ask her to marry me tonight," Thompkins said.

"Think she'll say yes?"

"I sure hope so. It'll be a lot easier being gone knowing she's waiting for me." He turned to Robert. "Thank you, sir. I appreciate your speaking out for the cause." He hurried ahead to join the pretty girl.

Robert watched him go. He thought about the Methodist Preacher's army commission. He remembered his own words about 'states' rights,' really meaning the right to subjugate other human beings for economic gain. Stopping that was a worthy endeavor. Since he was between churches, it suddenly loomed as an opportunity.

Robert turned for home. He wondered if Huggins' daughter would say yes. Since her church no longer had a minister, he guessed she'd have to be married by his friend, the Methodist Preacher. Robert felt some of the weight lift from his shoulders. He thanked God for the gift of his calling. Joining the army deserved more consideration, but the thought of it seemed to be settling in pretty comfortably—a worthy calling.

THE END

Sarge, STANDOFF

After his brief discussion with Private Strawberry Johnson, Union Army Sergeant Madison Jones remained on the knoll and watched three soldiers approach. They had reached a narrow path in the high grass out of the old-growth pines. Jones was disheartened to have lost a man. He recognized two of the three arrivals. Young, barely twenty, Private Curtis was tall, walked with a stiff-kneed gait, and habitually scanned the area around him. The shorter, Private Emory, was but a wisp of a man and took almost two steps to Curtis' one. They had carried the body of one of their comrades down the mountain to company head-quarters that morning. He didn't recognize the third man who led the procession. He was older, a bit taller than Emory, and stouter. But he tramped along the trail with assurance. The man's sun-faded uniform and Corporal stripes suggested that he had been in the infantry for a while. Sarge tightened his lips with approval. He could use another steady hand. He noted that the Corporal tramped up the slope, rising toward Sarge's position as energetically as the younger men!

Sarge extended his hand. "Sergeant Jones, Corporal."

"Nice to meet you, Sarge." The man took off his cap and swiped at the sweat on his forehead with a bandana. "I'm Robert Gracey. I'm the replacement for the young man the boys carried out this morning." He looked around and smiled toward the two younger men as they passed to join Strawberry and their other comrades in the shade of the trees. Sarge overheard someone query them about the new man.

"You go by Robert?"

"I do, and I don't, Sarge. You're welcome to call me Robert or Preacher. That was my calling before joining the army. Someday, I hope it will be again."

The information regarding the man's occupation didn't conjure up much confidence in the fighting department. Preacher? Sarge eyed the man's Corporal chevrons. "How long have you been in the army?"

Preacher followed Sarge's eyes down at his double stripes. "Not as long as you'd suspect, judging by those. It's been a year last month. To tell the truth, I enlisted with a group of boys, and when it came to promotion, I suspect it was an age before beauty decision." He smiled good-naturedly, exposing wide-gapped teeth. His bushy eyebrows raised a bit. Preacher flipped his cap back and forth by the little brim as if to dry it out some. He was four inches shorter than Sarge. Both his arms and legs were muscular, more suggestive of a working man than a clergyman.

"Preacher it is," Sarge sighed. He was a little disappointed with the man's history. "You fellas got here just in time. Our scout says five Rebels are holding up in a cabin about a mile from here. Cody, the scout we lost, and the redhead we call Strawberry, ran across them. Unfortunately, they saw Cody before he saw them."

"Based on the headcount, we have the odds in our favor then," Preacher said.

"Not exactly. Strawberry says they have a woman with them. But, from the swearing and carrying on he says he heard, she's not getting along with them too well."

"So, what's our play?"

"Not sure yet. I want to look the situation over for myself. You ready to go?"

"Yep. Lead on, Sergeant!" Preacher gave his big head and neck another swipe with the bandana and donned his cap.

Sarge moved toward the half dozen men and pulled them in close enough that he didn't have to shout. He knew that Rebels had scouts too. The men all knew the situation with the cabin as Strawberry had already filled them in.

"Boys, we're going to move in closer to the cabin. Keep your heads up and your distance. These big pines are a perfect cover for an ambush. Strawberry, you're still point man. Don't trust anything."

The small red-haired Private nodded. Strawberry stood, pulled on his pack, and seemed to adjust something under his coat, then led the way out of camp with his rifle in hand. Something about his movement was familiar. Preacher looked quizzically at Sarge.

"Armor?"

Sarge nodded. "His mother sent it to him a month ago. More to carry, but she thought it might save his life. I hope he doesn't get to test it."

Preacher had seen the thin iron or steel chest protectors before. Though advertised as impenetrable, they were anything but reliable. He had inspected one of the two-piece chest contraptions once. It was heavy and obviously not up to the task of stopping a hornet. Moreover, they were hot, uncomfortable, and very often abandoned during battle. But even the slim possibility of saving a life kept the manufacturers in business.

The Corporal nodded. "I'm with you. And I hope it doesn't tempt him to take any unnecessary chances."

Sarge grimaced at that remark. He pointed to the third position in line and motioned for Preacher to precede him. He wanted to get a read on the new man. One by one, the men lined up to follow along with about five paces between them. Sarge waved in the three sentinels to take rearguard positions. Thirty minutes later, Sarge and Preacher edged up close to Strawberry to look at the topography surrounding the cabin. It sat in a clearing about twenty-five yards back from a little bluff that ran across the cabin's front side and looked out on tree-covered switchbacks. A stream descended from higher up the mountainside and ran swiftly about thirty feet to the far side of the cabin. Sarge anticipated that the sound of the rushing water would help cover the movement of his men. He surmised that the small structure, rough and spare, had probably been built by trappers in the remote past. The little building had a small open window on the near side, and through it, they caught a glimpse of at least one window on the front. They could make out quarrelsome voices inside. The door leading out to a sagging porch had been left open. Keeping to the timber, they moved around to a point where they could see two men lounging on the porch.

Sarge spotted a third man, likely a sentinel at the far edge of the clearing, filling his canteen. The men's varied Confederate apparel suggested that at least two of them might be deserters. It didn't matter. One of them had put a bullet in Private Cody. That was enough to justify a full-fledged assault if it came to that.

"Ideas?" Sarge looked at Preacher.

"Well, the woman complicates things." Preacher murmured as he raised up a bit. His eyes followed the game trail that continued from their position and followed the terrain down the left side toward the bluff. Then, about ten yards further on, it veered to the right and out of sight. Sarge watched Preacher's face as he assessed the situation.

"You know it looks like a couple of men could follow this game trail around that bluff, climb up to the top and target the porch with good cover," Preacher said. "Of course, they'd have to take care of the lookout on the way. A man is sitting down there leaning against a tree just before the trail curves around."

"And?" Sarge's eyebrows raised slightly. He had not noticed the man.

Preacher tilted his big head back, squinted his eyes, and surveyed the rest of the area between the trees for a moment, then nodded to himself. "The rest of the men positioned along this game trail could put the porch in a crossfire. The thing is, if the shooting goes on long enough, the woman stands a good chance of catching a bullet."

"We could just surround them and tell them to give up," Sarge said. He looked toward Strawberry and the other men as if thinking the less shooting, the better, armor or no.

"But given time to think about it, mightn't they wonder what that woman was worth to us?" Preacher said.

"So, you think they might try to barter with her?" Sarge asked. "In that case, we'd have a standoff."

"Seems possible, what with them knowing what knights in shining armor we Union boys are." Preacher grinned.

Sarge's eyes flashed, and he nodded. He rubbed his chin. "You're thinking about shooting from that bluff, and the game trail gives me an idea." He could see now that the man on the ground leaning back against a tree had his hat tipped down low on his forehead as if dozing.

Sarge beckoned Strawberry to come over and pointed out the man. The Private nodded and motioned for Curtis and Emory to follow him. The men quickly skirted the left side of the clearing through the trees without being noticed. Strawberry moved ahead alone and dispatched the sleeping guard with the butt of his rifle. The inert body pitched forward and slid down the hill out of sight. The men continued to the far side of the bluff, then climbed up to a position where they could draw a bead on the men on the porch. Sarge, Preacher, and the remaining men prepared to assemble at the backside of the cabin when the shooting by its inhabitants started.

Sarge watched as Private Strawberry stood in plain view for an instant and fired a hurried shot that sent both men on the porch skittering into the cabin, slamming the door behind them. As instructed, all three Union soldiers then peppered the front of the house, avoiding the two windows. Once inside, the Rebels immediately directed a steady stream of lead toward the area where Strawberry and the other two men had commenced their fire. The man by the stream hunched down and joined in.

Once the Rebel started firing back, Strawberry and his two companions, following Sarge's orders, backed down the bluff and hightailed it back up the trail under cover of the trees to take up new positions where they could fire across the porch. As instructed, they held their fire. Meanwhile, Sarge, Preacher, and the rest of the men scrambled to the rear of the cabin, where they waited.

It didn't take long for the men inside to realize that no one was shooting back. Several minutes elapsed, interrupted by the sound of a mumbled conversation inside the little house. Impatient, a burly middle-aged man was the first to edge out of the door to assess the silence. He leaped off the front of the porch and threw himself down behind a large stump. The silence continued for a bit. Then another man stuck his head out and hollered toward the cliff.

"We got us a woman in here. Come any closer, and we plug her." He moved to stand halfway through the door. He pulled the woman into the doorway. Sarge and Preacher eyed one another when they heard a muffled yell and a stream of feminine swearing from the woman. The silence continued atop the abandoned cliff. Peeking out around the far edge of the cabin, Sarge could see that the man behind the stump seemed to grow impatient as well. He finally stood and took a couple of tentative steps toward the bluff. He made a ready target if Sarge had been looking for one, but that could spoil the plan. The man walked forward some more and grew bolder as he approached the ledge without attracting fire. The man by the stream followed close behind.

"I don't think there's anybody here, Pete!" Following his shout, two other men cautiously exited the cabin and joined them. There were now four men along the ledge. They gazed off in the distance as if the Union shooters might have flown away. Finally, another man came out with an older woman tagging along after him. She started to speak, but he hushed her and pushed her back inside before pulling the door closed. He cautiously joined the other men at the cliff's edge. They milled about for a moment before Sarge moved away from the side of the cabin and announced himself.

"You men drop your weapons!" Sarge shouted. The Rebels whirled around. Pete's men were lined up like targets at a shooting gallery. They could see multiple guns aimed at them from covered positions. "Drop them! This is your last chance!" Sarge called. After a moment calculating the odds, Pete lowered his rifle to the ground.

"Handguns too," Sarge commanded. Strawberry and his two companions stepped out of the trees. The realization that they were covered on two sides seemed to convince the other men. As they discarded their weapons, Sarge motioned to Strawberry and two other young men to gather them up.

Preacher stepped up on the porch. Then, keeping his rifle ready, he felt behind him for the door and opened it. "You can come out now, ma am. It's alright."

To Preacher's surprise, the snout of a shotgun poked out first. The woman followed it. The double barrels stabbed Preacher between his shoulder blades. "Now, you and your men drop your guns," she called toward Sarge. Preacher turned his head and eyed her, trying to reassess the situation. He guessed the woman to be in her fifties. Clearly, she was not a hostage. Her eyes were hot with fear and hatred.

"All you Yankees, drop your guns, or I'll blow this Corporal to smithereens." Though her voice shook a little, her face was resolute.

The men along the ledge let out a shout of glee and advanced to retrieve their weapons. With his squad members' lives in jeopardy, Sarge knew he had no choice but to call her bluff. He fired a round into the ground in front of them. He gritted his teeth, hoping he would not hear an answering blast from the shotgun. "Keep those boys in your sights, men," Sarge ordered. If she drops Preacher, shoot all of them." Sarge turned his rifle toward the woman and waited for her response.

Preacher gingerly edged around to face the woman. He felt the double barrels brush his back, his arm, and then rest against his chest. He looked into the woman's anxious eyes. Finally, he spoke apologetically, "Ma'am, we don't fancy shooting a woman, but if you pull that trigger, my friends are going to be obliged to shoot you and all of your boys."

Preacher glanced around as Strawberry and the other two men continued their errand of gathering the remaining weapons. They were now piled on the edge of the porch. Suddenly there was the bark of a rifle from the edge of the game trail. In the commotion, they had forgotten the man Strawberry had knocked out. Now revived and ignorant of the state of the negotiations, he rose and fired his rifle as if to end the stand-off. There was a metallic whacking sound as the man's bullet struck Strawberry in the chest. The red-headed soldier spun around from the impact and fell to the ground. Instinctively,

Sarge swung his rifle around and fired on the man. His bullet caught him in the leg. He went down with a yelp of pain.

Sarge looked back toward the women. He could see her face work. For a moment, he thought she might turn her shotgun on him. "Jeb!" Her eyes registered stark panic. She hesitated for but a moment, pulled the gun away and was off the porch at a run.

Sarge motioned for two of his men to follow and disarm her while he and Preacher hurried to Strawberry's side. The young redhead was lying on his back. There was a hole in his coat just below the first button. Sarge felt a surge of dread. He pulled open the garment to expose the armor. There was a dime-sized hole in a crater where the two halves overlapped.

"Damnit!" Sarge straightened and kicked the earth in disgust. "Damnit to hell!"

Then miraculously, the boy's eyes fluttered. The hedge of reddish eyebrows quivered, and his hand stirred to reach toward his chest. Silently he slid his forefinger into the hole and groaned. "Boy, that took the wind out of me!"

"What the!" Preacher helped the soldier sit up. Strawberry struggled as if trying to remove the coat. Sarge couldn't fathom how the boy could be alive. Free of his jacket, Strawberry pulled one of the iron plates away from this chest and reached in behind it. He fumbled around a bit to pull out a thick object. It was a book familiar to them all. He opened the Bible to reveal a round trapped halfway through. Preacher read the verse where the round had stopped.

"Put on the whole armor of God...with the breastplate of righteousness in place...," Preacher whispered and twisted around and looked at Sarge. "Ephesians 5:13 or thereabouts." Then he found

his voice. "There's a sermon here, somewhere, I bet!" Preacher's hand patted the young man's shoulder and grinned.

"If one doesn't stop a hornet, the other will, it seems." Sarge smiled and helped Strawberry to his feet. "So was the Bible your momma's idea too?"

"She said they were a set," Strawberry grinned back.

"Momma bears always protect their cubs," Preacher said. He motioned toward the downed Rebel and the mother ministering to his wound.

Sarge looked thoughtfully at his cool-headed Corporal. He now knew something important about him as well.

THE END

Pappy, MISSION IN TEXAS

Sergeant Matthew (Pappy) Jordon lay deep in the Texas arroyo with seven other men. After an ambush, they were stranded without their horses ten miles from their home base, a small Spanish mission twenty miles north of San Antonio. In the lull between volleys from the Mexicans, Matthew wondered if he'd ever see his farm in Harlon County, Georgia, again. His elderly neighbor, Captain Fredrick Ingerstall Senior, was to his left. The officer's wounded arm was suspended in a makeshift sling while his free hand was caressing the thinning curls on his son's head. His son, Fredrick Junior, Matthew's best friend, was dead. They could all be dead eventually for lack of water if the Mexicans didn't get them first. The soldiers who had them pinned down commanded the only source of water for miles. The outlook for the Union troopers seemed desperate.

Matthew, at forty-nine, had received his aged-sounding nickname from his son, Howie, when the boy was but a toddler. It lingered among his friends even after the boy began to call him

Dad. Matthew was a year younger than the Colonel's lifeless son. He glanced at his friend's ashen features for a moment, and then his eyes moved to Privates Gerald Henson and Scotty Harrison. Wisely, the two were keeping their heads down. The wounded Captain and inert son served as reminders of the cost if they abandoned caution. Matthew and Fred had been friends ever since their families settled farms near one another over twenty years before. Whereas Matthew was small and slight of built, Fred had once stood tall like his father.

When Fred Junior had proposed the venture six months before, Matthew knew that he had no business trotting off to Texas to fight Mexicans. He had already fought Creek Indians for longer than he could stomach, and they had actually been a threat to hearth and home.

But Fredrick Senior was going, either alone or with an escort. Born in 1778, just three years before the end of the Revolutionary War, the senior Ingerstall grew up amid the patriotic stories of glory that followed his country's independence. Events had prevented him from participating in the War of 1812 against the British until the last six months of 1815. He felt cheated when the war ended. So, when Georgia organized a brigade to fight the Mexicans in Texas, Ingerstall insisted, despite ample evidence to the contrary, that he was up to the task of commanding one of the six companies. Fred was Matthew's friend, and the man was concerned about his sixty-nine-year-old father taking off for Texas on his own. The deciding factor for Matthew was that by going, he'd have a good reason to deny his twenty-six-year-old son, Howie, the privilege. Someone had to take care of the farm. Ingerstall's elderly slave, Isaiah, could be trusted to run their farm during both Ingerstalls' absence. Matthew owned no slaves.

The laughter carried by the wind across the dry plain made it evident that the enemy planned to stick around until the gringos were dead. Matthew watched as the Captain's hand absently stroked his dead son's head while he stared at the sky toward the wisps of smoke rising from the Mexicans' campfire. Matthew wondered what the older man was thinking. Could the Captain be as filled with self-loathing as Matthew for his own decision to come?

After hours of stalemate, the Mexicans were toying with them now. One of them would fire his old flintlock every half hour or so to keep them worried. Matthew knew that if they chose, the Mexicans could wait until they died of dehydration. The men in the arroyo could feel the sun and heat sucking the life out of them even while their water held out. Now it was all gone, for the last canteen passed around two hours before was empty. After that, there would be no more water. Matthew imagined a picnic-like atmosphere among the willows and cottonwood trees. Someone was strumming a guitar. By the sound of it, they had started to celebrate their victory early.

"Matthew." Captain Ingerstall ignored the formalities with his deceased son's best friend. "Got any ideas?"

"We're done for, sir," Matthew blurted. Then seeing the shocked expressions on the faces of the two younger men, he amended his declaration. "We're done for without water. They know it, and we know it. They probably figure that we'll go crazy and come charging out of this hole eventually, and they'll pick us off with those old muskets they're carrying. Our cap locks are no advantage today." He paused. His little recitation wasn't telling the older man anything new. They needed a plan. A good plan, and soon!

The Mexicans had food, water, shade, ammunition, and horses. The Americans had ammunition and maybe a biscuit in a pocket that they'd choke on without something with which to wash it down. So, what was missing from the equation?

"Sir, the only way out of here is stealing horses. I don't have an idea about doing that just yet." He added the "just yet," almost as an afterthought. He could see the words gave the younger men some hope. But he kicked himself some; for now, they'd all expect him to come up with a plan. There was that word, "plan," again!

Dusk was coming on. Further down the creek, Private Jeffs had a coughing fit. Private Marrs, sunburned and seemingly more dehydrated than the others, had started to mumble to himself. The old Captain just sat silently and stroked his son's head. Matthew wondered bitterly if the corpse would eventually have a bald spot. There was no moon rising as yet. Matthew tried to remember if there should be. His Farmer's Almanac in his saddlebags might amuse the foe with the drawings for a little while. He looked at the sky. Stars overhead without the moon would do little to light their surroundings. Matthew shifted to one side to look around a large sage bush at the top of the bank. The countryside was dotted with the native sage, which varied from two to six feet tall. Matthew's mind churned through the prospects. Given sufficient tequila, the Mexicans might lose patience with their death vigil and attack in the darkness. If that happened, the many sage bushes in front of him would provide good cover for them. Maybe after darkness fell, he should send some of the men out to cut out the nearby plants and drag them away from the line of fire?

As darkness descended, the features of Matthew's men faded into dark lavender, then ever-deepening shades of gray. Finally, he decided it was dark enough to walk down the gully and check on everyone. Both Marrs and Jeffs were asleep. Giles and Smith were whispering to each other. They grabbed their handguns when they heard Matthew approach.

"Easy, men," the Sergeant whispered. He peaked over the arroyo's bank. There was nothing to be seen except sage and sand.

"Sergeant, we're not going to get out of this, are we?" Giles said.

"I told you, Sergeant Jordon will think of something," Corporal Smith answered for him.

Matthew felt the ire rise again at the man's words. He couldn't think of anything in his history that would suggest that out of eight men, he would be more likely to develop a solution than any of the others. But, of course, Matthew did pride himself on making good decisions. Better decisions than the one that had landed him in this godforsaken hell-hole in Texas. But sometimes, there were no solutions. Maybe there was no solution to take them out of the spot they were in now?

"The Mexicans might come in the dark," he said, leaving the man's question unanswered. "Try and stay alert. In another couple of hours, they might get drunk enough to get careless and charge us."

They nodded, but they were tired, almost hopeless nods. Matthew was leaving their desire for a good idea unrequited. He moved forward to Private Johnson, another of his neighbors in Harlon County. He was scrunched down in a ball. Matthew lay his hand on the man's shoulder, and the twenty-year-old jerked alert. He grabbed Matthew's wrist in a defensive motion, letting out a low cry that carried further than the older man would have liked.

"Easy, son," Matthew whispered. He poked his head up and surveyed the area from Johnson's vantage point. In the darkness, the sage bushes were as visually impenetrable as a boulder. Using the sage for cover, the Mexicans could be on them before anyone noticed! Matthew felt a chill run through him. He pictured the aftermath of such a raid. Eight men sprawled lifeless in the morning sun; the Captain's old bald noggin translucent with a bullet through it, his hand in mid-stroke on his son's flaxen head.

The Sergeant turned and took in the scene on the backside of the dry creek. All he could make out was more sage. Should they run? How far could they go through that near-desert without horses? Without water? Starting now, how far could they travel before the sun breached the eastern horizon? Not nearly far enough! The Mexicans had water, horses, and time on their side. Even if they didn't strike in the night, they would always have the advantage.

Matthew let himself sink back against the bank and stare up at the stars. He tried to think of some way to change the equation. Weren't all problems just equations in the end? He badly needed to change at least one of the many factors around in their favor. Which one?

The Sergeant dozed for a while despite his worry, for he was as tired as the others. When he shook his head awake, there was an anxiety-ridden, last-chance idea lingering on the edge of his senses. He stood and walked the length of the creek, searching the surrounding sand and rock. As he came to each of the men, he shook them awake and whispered, "follow me." By the time he rejoined the Captain, his desperate plan was complete.

"Sir, I have an idea." Matthew ducked down close to the older man's face. He sensed a flicker of a smile on the weathered features though he couldn't see it.

"Good." The Captain's hand came away from his stroking, and he ran his fingers over the white stubble on his chin. His head turned to take in the black outlines of the others now gathered close and waited.

Matthew explained his notion. Since he could not see well enough to read their expressions, he ran over the plan again to ensure that they understood. There were no questions, nor did anyone fault it. At best, there was a collective shrug. Matthew suspected that knowing it was their only chance gave rise to stoic acceptance regardless of merit.

"Do all of you have a timepiece?" Matthew pulled his watch and angled it to catch as much starlight as possible. "Okay, it is almost one o'clock. In an hour, at two, light things up and skedaddle. Remember, the Mexican camp will likely be an anthill of men running in all directions once we rost them. For God's sake, try not to shoot each other!" Matthew patted each man on the back, in turn, to send them off on their missions. Everything depended on their not being detected getting to their positions.

"After the last man departed, Matthew turned to Captain Ingerstall. Unfortunately, Sir, we can't take, Fred."

"I know." The old Captain lurched painfully to his feet. "And I can't leave without him."

Matthew felt the bile rise again. He was sure that however successful his idea might be, the odds were poor that there could be a return trip for father and son. Captain Ingerstall's comment acknowledged that.

"Yes, sir." He saluted Fred Senior and patted Fred Junior's shoulder for the last time. Then, he climbed the bank and crawled toward a tall sage bush fifty feet away. He squatted behind it and looked to his left and right. He thought he might catch a glimpse of one of the other men but saw nothing. Good!

Matthew hunkered down when he was within sixty yards of the Mexican's camp and tried to see where the sentinels had stationed themselves. Earlier, with the campfire blazing brightly, the men had cast long shadows into the night. Now, the fire was but a few red embers. There was no movement. Eight men against twenty were impossible odds in a fair fight. The Americans couldn't afford a fair fight. That was the equation that Matthew's plan sought to change.

The Sergeant tilted his watch again. Fifteen minutes remained. Closer to the stream, willow trees predominated the near landscape. But there were three large cottonwood trees on the Mexican camp's side of the water. Matthew bet that one of the trees would offer a welcome object for a sentinel to lean against. Quickly he was again in motion heading toward the leafy blackness.

As he crawled, Matthew estimated the time and how close they were to the moment of truth. He moved slowly, stopping every few feet to listen. Then, at last, as he neared the closest cottonwood, he heard the sound of heavy breathing. But it was out of sync. That puzzled him for a moment before he realized that two sentinels were leaning back against the same tree. Now the time was truly critical. Matthew went to his knees and hurried forward. He calculated that he had but a few minutes remaining. Two sleeping men were separated from most of the camp's occupants by at least a hundred feet or more. Soldiering requires a hardened heart. Matthew touched the handle of the knife that was prodding his midsection. He forced his resolve to rise over conscience. His belly lurched as he slid the blade from the sheath. Seconds! Then these two men would awaken with the rest of the camp for sure. Matthew slipped in close and swiftly made a slicing motion with the knife. The blade glided across the first and then the second man's jugular as quietly as a snake through the grass. Mid snore, silence, then a gurgle, then silence again. The odds shifted from eight against twenty to eight against eighteen.

Two o'clock! Suddenly there were sparks of light! There were five simultaneous fires lit in an arc from left to right behind him. The flames sputtered for mere seconds as the first piles of highly combustible green sage caught fire and roared into small infernos. Matthew looked behind him. He could see nothing but flames leaping skyward. In the camp, horses screamed in fear. Men jumped to their feet with their guns drawn. Shouted words in Spanish filled the air, and the Mexican soldiers waved their weapons at each other and motioned toward the fires. Where were the gringos? Were they under attack?

The Sergeant held his breath. Would the Mexicans run toward the fires or away? In their panic, they did both. The Union men were lying flat in the sand as far forward of the fires as they could manage after ignition. With the flames behind them, they were invisible to the Mexicans. The Mexican soldiers who elected to rush toward the flames were easy targets. A shot rang out. A second. Then fear took hold, and shots rang with abandon. While the sage was burning mightily, Matthew tried to see behind him, but he was as blinded by the flames as the Mexicans. The Sergeant turned as a man ran toward him from his left, his rifle at the ready. The two found each other in the flickering light at the same instant. This time Matthew's conscience did not slow him. He swung his handgun around and fired from five feet away. The bullet found its mark before the Mexican could bring his flintlock to his shoulder. The odds shifted. Now they were eight to seventeen. Other guns fired to the left and right of him. The Sergeant knew the odds were changing with almost every explosion of gunpowder. But were they changing in his favor? That, he couldn't know, so his thoughts turned to the horses!

Matthew headed through the shelter of the willows to the excited animals. He could see that some were hobbled when he arrived, but most were merely tied to the small willows that lined the bank. Several Mexican soldiers were mounting horses bareback. Two men were attempting to saddle horses. He approached one of the men from behind just as he prepared to mount. Matthew's knife plunged deep into the Mexican's side.

Quickly he grabbed the reins and pulled the horse along as he gathered two more.

In the arroyo, Captain Ingerstall peered up over the bank's edge at the fiery display. Sergeant Jordon rode up and shouted a warning. "I'm coming in, Captain! It's Matthew. I have horses! Matthew slid to the ground and noted that the fires were beginning to burn out. More horses approached. Somehow all of the men had remembered Matthew's caution to use the North Star to orient themselves.

"Help me with Fred, Johnson." Matthew and the bigger man threw the body over the horse's back. He turned to assist Fred Senior to one of the saddled animals. "Everyone here?" The gunshots continued in the camp. Were they shooting each other, or did they have some of his men penned down? He didn't know. "Who's here?" He called again.

"Here, Sergeant," Jeffs and then Marrs chimed in.

"Here," Smith yelped. Jerald and Scotty spoke up then.

"Everybody?" Matthew could scarcely believe it. He found the North Star, reined his horse north toward the Spanish Mission, where the rest of their company camped. He looked back toward the smoldering brush fires and the camp beyond. The shouting continued behind them, but there was no gunfire. Each plunging step of his Mexican horse took him further from the blood and death, but he doubted that any distance could erase the memory of this night. As the first light brightened the eastern horizon, the Sergeant wondered if the death of Fredrick Ingerstall's son left the old Captain with the same bitterness as the loss of his friend did him. How could it not? For himself, Matthew knew that he would never speak of his part in this war. He overheard

Private Jeffs telling Marrs that Sergeant Jordon was a hero. He pushed the thought aside. Being a hero would just bring more questions, more details, more memories of a knife's swift thrust, a pistol's flames lighting a dead man's face. They were bitter memories that he hoped time would fade.

THE END

Bronco, BRONCO GOES TO WAR

The dew was thick on that May morning 1864. The three Union Privates were up at daybreak. They were camped twenty yards off the road, north of Elizabethtown, Kentucky, where they'd catch a train for Chattanooga, Tennessee. As they traveled, the morning chores had evolved into something of a ritual. Bronco, the second oldest of the three, was the first to arise. He slapped away the crushed leaves clinging to his shirt and pants. He was tall, lean, and erect. He had a mop of brown hair protruding from his Union cap over his straight, firmly set nose. Mutton-chop sideburns extended almost to his jawline. He had adopted the style upon entry into the service, but the new growth was already fretting him. Like the others, he wore a Union cap and uniform. A keen-eyed marksman, Bronco smiled with satisfaction as he checked his rifle and went off in search of game without a word to either of his companions.

Frank, the oldest, arose just as the sound of Bronco's footsteps subsided. He walked in the opposite direction and looked for kindling for the fire. Frank was as tall as Bronco, two years older and a little heavier. He was the son of a farmer back in Ohio. His eyes were a darker, cloudier blue than those of the younger man. He had worked for a horse trader before joining the army. He had talked Bronco into joining up with him to be a wrangler. He knew the Army needed wranglers, he said. But, as it turned out, that expectation didn't work out for either of them. The Army needed foot soldiers more than wranglers, it seemed. So though Frank humorously claimed he could sell sawdust to a lumber mill, he couldn't buck the orders that put him and Bronco in the infantry. Their orders weren't even for the same outfit.

Bud, the youngest of the three, whistled low to himself as he threw off his blanket and stooped to his knees to start preparations for breakfast. Bud was shorter than the other two men and about two years younger than Bronco. He was stout from muscle rather than fat and brown-eyed. His hands were big with thick fingers. He nursed the coals into a flicker of flame and slid in a couple of sticks leftover from the previous night. His ears were attentive for the report of Bronco's rifle. The men much preferred Bronco's rabbits over the biscuits the army gave them when they had headed out a few days before.

Bronco had not gone far when he encountered a rocky area. There were huge mounds of sandstone standing sidewise as if a giant plow had passed through the countryside, upending great slabs of earth and mantle. An ominous sound awakened him from his thoughts. He stood still and listened. Again, he picked up the rattling sound. Bronco peered around but could see nothing. There was no mistaking the sound of a rattlesnake. There was a house-sized rock outcropping ahead and just a trace of a game trail around it. He walked forward carefully on the balls of his feet, prepared to jump in any direction should he spot the source of the sound.

Rounding the boulder, he spied a small black man sitting on a slab of stone. A young black boy sat on a low ledge a few feet away from him with his feet drawn up to his chin. The man held a five-foot-long cane branch in front of him with a small hook on one end. The length of the cane in proportion to the height of the man told Bronco that it wasn't a walking cane. Instead, it reminded him more of a shepherd's crook but shorter than any he had ever seen before. He looked around and saw no sign of sheep. Then a movement in the corner of his eye drew his attention back to the man who moved the stick left to right and back in a steady motion that reminded Bronco of divining for water. In a flash, a long diamond-backed snake sprang from the ground and struck at the rod. The sound and lightning-quick movement made Bronco's hair stand on end.

Bronco took a step back and searched the ground around him to ensure that there were no snakes in his immediate vicinity. It seemed safe. He stepped forward again, and in doing so, his shoe struck a glancing blow on a loose rock, causing it to tumble into another. The sound caught the boy and the man's attention. The man looped the snake in his staff and looked around. Seeing Bronco, he grinned.

"You caught me funning the snake." He said. He had a bit of an accent that Bronco couldn't place.

"Isn't that a rattlesnake?" To Bronco, it did not seem like an appealing playmate.

"Yes. Where we just come from, they are called timber rattlers."

"That is a big snake. It looks to be at least five feet long."

"Yes, sir. This is a big'un." He stood up as Bronco approached. The long snake partially wrapped itself around the staff. The head hung off a foot and a half. It contracted a bit as if preparing to spring again.

The man pointed toward a gunny sack by his foot. "I've already got three in there. I was debating whether to add this one when you came along."

"What are you going to do with them?" Bronco moved cautiously forward a step.

"Well, me and the young'un were planning to eat them. Haven't you ever eaten snake?"

"I've heard of it. What do snakes taste like?"Meat was meat, but Bronco was not sure about snakes.

"Well, it depends on how you cook it and what spices you use. It usually falls somewhere between chicken and fish." He moved the staff a bit to push the snake out toward the end. Its rattles were going crazy.

Bronco looked around again. "Dang! I've heard snakes come in pairs?"

"Well, that can be true. I found two of the three fellers in the sack close together, though I don't know that they were a couple." He grinned. "So, do you want this one?"

"Well, I'm traveling with two friends. I don't know if they'd be interested in snake or not." Bronco looked doubtful.

"Are you camped by the road?" The little man asked. "I'll tell you what; let's go up and ask them." He pulled a knife from his boot and pinned the snake down with the cane. Then, with a motion too fast for Bronco to see, he took the head off the snake with a single flick of his wrist. They watched it writhe on the ground for a few seconds and then lie still. Finally, the man picked it up and dropped it in the sack.

"First, let's go clean and wash them." He motioned downhill, and Bronco followed close behind, keeping his eyes open for more snakes. Finally, they arrived at a pool fed by runoff from the recent rain. "My name is Bronco Brumley." Bronco stuck out his hand, and the little man shook it. His hand was leaner and smaller than Broncos. The pinky finger was missing making it seem like a child's hand in size when they shook.

"Folks call me Bert." The little man grinned, showing white teeth and crinkly furrows around his eyes. Bronco guessed he was in his late twenties, several years older than himself. He wore a slouch hat on the back of his head. His clothes were old and worn. "This boy is Willy." The black boy stepped forward and extended his tiny hand. He was almost as tall as Bert. He was bright-eyed and confident-looking for a fifteen-year-old. Bert pulled his knife again,

"I'll show you how to skin and clean a snake, okay?"

"Sure." Bronco edged forward to watch.

The snake he had just killed was still moving, so Bert pulled one of the limp snakes from the burlap bag and stretched it out to about four feet in length. Bert lay the snake in the grass and started at the place where he had severed the head. He then ran the blade about a quarter-inch deep the entire length of the snake. He used his thumb to slide down the gully he had created to remove all the guts and other internal organs. He let the innards fall in the grass to one side. Then he stood up, pulled at the skin until he had enough loose to grasp with all three of his fingers and thumb. He alternated pulling and moving his anchor hand down the snake's length until the skin fell away in one long strip. Bert dunked the long fleshy body into the rushing water to wash off the blood and scraps. He swished it about for a moment and pulled it out with a flourish. "Good eatin'!" he proclaimed with a grin. Willy nodded his head in agreement. Bert repeated the process and then looked at Bronco questioningly.

"Do you want to try one?" Bert asked.

Bronco lay down his Henry rifle and accepted the third snake. He had cleaned a lot of rabbits and several hundred fish in his life. This chore did not seem that much different aside from knowing that the snake could have caused an agonizing death just a few minutes before.

Bronco had killed snakes many times but had never handled any, so the snake's smooth yet scaley feel in his hands was a new sensation. Bert handed him the knife, and Bronco ran it down the length of his snake. After stripping out the inside, he handed the knife back and worked to get a handhold while he started pulling the skin. It was a lot like cleaning fish. He dropped it in the water and retrieved it. Bert quickly finished the last snake and dropped it in immediately after his. "Do you eat snakes a lot?" Bronco asked as Bert retrieved the four critters.

"Well, while we have been traveling, about once or twice a week. We like to change up with rabbits, turtles, and terrapins. Rabbits are harder to catch, but you can do it in the very early morning." Bert rinsed out the sack. He put the snakes inside and stood up. "So, maybe your friends will like snake meat?"

"Like I said, I don't know. They both like rabbits well enough." Bronco smiled. "We'll know in a minute!" They headed up toward the road.

As Bronco appeared at the edge of the camp, Bud looked up. "I didn't hear your rifle, so I guess it's biscuits for us this ….?" He stopped mid-sentence when he spotted Bert and Willy bringing up the rear.

"Well, what do you think of rattlesnake for a change, Bud?" Bronco turned to the little black man who grinned. "This is Bert and Willy. We've got four rattlers to try out if you're interested."

"Well, that sounds great." Bud cut in. "I've eaten rattlers before. They sure beat biscuits." He glanced toward Frank.

"Never tried it," Frank responded. "Is it pretty good?"

"Well, like I said, it beats biscuits." Bud extended his hand and shook Willey's three fingers, then the boy's hand.

Bert looked around. "Any chance you have a frying pan?"

Frank shook his head. "No, too heavy to lug around. I guess we'll have to cut it into pieces and put it on a spit like we do rabbit."

Bert wrinkled his nose and sighed. "Skillets are heavy to pack. I don't carry one either." He grabbed the headless end of one of the snakes out of the sack and lopped off about five inches. "You need to cut at an angle with the ribs, so you don't have any loose bones," he said. He handed a piece to Bud, who dug into his bag and pulled out two containers. He rubbed some salt and pepper into the flesh and threaded it onto a spit. They repeated the process until they had four spits over the hot coals. In a few minutes, the meat was sizzling and bubbling. Bert handed Willy a chunk, and the boy took a bite, quickly slipping the meat from the bones. Each of the soldiers pulled off a piece, blew on it, and tasted gingerly.

"Not bad," Frank pronounced, and they proceeded to finish off most of the meat with enthusiasm. Then, after a few minutes, Frank voiced his final opinion. "Well," he said as he leaned back. "It's a little tougher than a rabbit."

"Yes, that's because hanging it over a fire cooks it too fast," Bert said. "For tender snake meat, it is best to bake it. You can also add different spices."

"I notice a lilt in your voice that I haven't heard before. Kind of British but still different." Frank looked at Bert, who smiled.

"Yes, I am from Jamaica. A rich plantation owner in Alabama originally purchased me. "

"Where is Jamaica?" Bronco looked around the circle.

"A long way from here," Frank said. He looked at Bert, who was nodding his head in agreement.

"Yes, a very long way. I was a dock worker in Port Royal. My friends and I were making good money. One night we partied very late down by the waterfront and drank too much rum. We were kidnapped and brought to Mobile, where they sold us as slaves."

"I see you only have three fingers." Bronco ventured. He had hesitated to mention it before. He had been taught that it was impolite to point out a deformity, but he was still curious.

Bert held up his three-fingered hand. "One day two months after I arrived, while my owner's guards marched me through the market with some other men, I reached out to take a peach from a fruit stand. A guard grabbed me and threw me down and held me while another guard whipped me." Bert turned and lifted his shirt to show the healed welts. "When I continued to resist, he held me while another guard cut off this finger." Bert made a slicing motion.

The three men leaned forward. Bert showed the rough scar. "He used a dull knife and tore the tendons of the finger next to it." Bert took out his knife and ran his finger down the back of the blade. "I keep my knife very sharp, yes?" He flipped it with great agility and, holding it by the handle, sent it flying toward a nearby tree. It struck sharp end first and vibrated in place.

"Dang!" Bronco said, impressed. "So, you were not a slave in Jamaica?"

"No, I was a free man in Jamaica!" Bert said emphatically and drew himself up to his full height. I will never be a slave again. Slavery was abolished in Jamaica by the British before I was born, and my parents were freed. Until the men kidnapped me, I have always been free. I will never submit to slavery!" He jumped up and retrieved his knife. "But it is just as well that I came to America. In Jamaica, your standing in society is dependent on how light-skinned you are."

As you can see, I am quite dark. So, I would never be happy there. Mister Lincoln will finish slavery here. Willy and I are headed north for a good job and a better life." He put his hand on Willy's shoulder. "Willy was born a slave in Alabama. His mother got very sick. She found out I was planning to escape and asked me to take Willy with me." He patted the boy's shoulder. The boy looked at Bert with a trace of tears, thinking of his Mother. Bert pulled up the boy's shirt. Willy had welts as well. "All of this is over. Now we are going to be free men forever, right Willy?" The boy wiped his tears away, grinned, and nodded. Bronco tried to imagine being a slave and at the mercy of other men. He felt a mixture and alarm rise up. The experiences of these two men represented the real reason he wore the blue uniform.

Frank looked at the sun now well over the horizon. "We need to get on the road. We have a long hike ahead of us." He looked at his companions and stood up. The other men stood as well. "Are you traveling north?" he asked Bert.

"Yes. As long as we are in Confederate country, we will keep off the main roads as much as we can to avoid conflict with the slavers. Even this far north, there are a lot of them about. Some men in Rebel uniforms almost captured us before dark last night. We were lucky to get away. I do not carry a gun. It would just make us targets. I have just the knife. We live off the land. We will soon be far enough north, I think."

"How did you know you were safe with me," Bronco asked.

"You wear the blue uniform. Black folks in the south know the American flag and the blue uniform mean freedom." He smiled and gave each man a three-fingered handshake. "Good luck to you," he said to each man. In a moment, he and Willy were gone.

"I hope he makes it okay," Bronco said.

Frank nodded. "Seems like a smart feller. He may be a tad over-optimistic about the flag and uniform, though."

The men were about to head off when they heard a thrashing sound in the direction of the road. Willy burst through the undergrowth. His formerly calm eyes were wild with fear. "The bad men found us! They have Bert!"

"Who? Frank said.

"Rebels!"

"How many?" Bud asked.

"Three!" Willy pointed behind him. "They say they're going to hang him!"

The three men exchanged glances and grabbed up their rifles. Bronco motioned that he'd circle to the left. Frank and Bud followed Willy down the short trail toward the road. They could hear the rough voices of the men hurling threats at the little Jamaican. Peering around the foliage, they could see that a tall, big-boned man had already thrown a rope over the branch of an oak. He stood twirling the noose-end impatiently while his two smaller companions grew exasperated trying to subdue Bert. He kept eluding their attempts to loop a short rope around his wrists. Finally, one of the men leaned too far forward, and Bert head-butted him. That brought a burst of blood from his nose. He swore and pulled his gun while wiping his injured snout with the back of his hand. The blond-headed third man was just looking on. Seemly bored, he stepped away from the fight.

"Just shoot the little shit! I'll see if I can find that kid." He took a half dozen running steps and stopped abruptly. Frank and Bud's rifles were three feet from his belly. "Jack! We got company!" He tossed the words back at the other two men and raised his hands, but only elbow high as if not fully committed to surrender.

The thick-set man of about fifty sporting Sergeant stripes looked around. He swore under his breath. "Yankees, and pups at that!" He grabbed Bert by his hair and pulled his revolver. "Put your guns away, or I'll shoot him right now. three against two are pretty good odds."

Bronco could see Jack on the other side of the trail. Bronco silently edged around a large oak tree and sighted down his rifle. Though the man didn't know it, the odds were not as good as he thought. Bronco felt a twinge of apprehension, for he could be on the verge of killing a man for the first time in his life. It was enough to give him pause. Then, remembering that the lives of Bert and Willy were at risk, he pushed the thought aside. Jack would decide his own fate.

Frank grinned and leveled his rifle at the man as well. Then, he raised his chin and shouted at the world at large. "It's not three against two! Bronco, Bob, Nate, give him something to think about!" The Rebels looked around, startled at the possibility of more shooters.

Bronco's Henry rifle barked. The report was sharp in the still morning air, and the hornet whistled through Jack's hat. The two other men watched as the cap flew off and sailed between them. Jack hollered in pain and grabbed the top of his head. His fingers came away bloody. He hastily dropped the forty-four. Then, with Frank's point made, the other men's hands flew up in surrender.

Bud pulled the gun from the man standing before him, and they turned him back toward the others. Bronco walked up from the left, secretly pleased that he had been spared the need to kill the man. He motioned for the men to drop their guns.

Jack regained his hat and looked around. "Where are the others?"

Frank grinned. "I exaggerated."

Jack muttered something under his breath.

"Now, don't get fussy, Frank said. "This is a good situation to negotiate."

"There's nothing to negotiate, Jack said."

Frank grinned. "Of course, there is. There is always something to negotiate. For instance, instead of shooting you," he motioned with his rifle...."

"Or hanging you," Bronco said, catching Frank's drift and pointing toward the noose hanging slack from the limb.

"We'll take the horses and leave you alive with some rattlesnake meat to enjoy for breakfast."

Bronco nodded in agreement and grinned. "That's a fair trade!"

The four men glowered.

"Well, negotiations are over." Frank motioned Jack to join the others and whacked the man in the seat of his pants. "We're not going to steal your horses. I can't abide a thief." He grinned again. "We will merely borrow them until the war's over." He looked at Bert. "I'd invite you to ride with us, but we're going the opposite direction."

Bert grinned. "We go north and put men such as these behind us." Then, without more discussion, he and Willy disappeared into the trees again.

"Are infantrymen allowed to ride horses?" Bronco raised his eyebrows. He answered his own question. "Yes, I've heard of mounted infantrymen before." He smiled and reverently put his hands on the horse closest to him. It nickered as he breathed in the animal's aroma. "And I love horses!"

THE END

John Coates, THE ESCAPE

August 1840. Fourteen-year-old Johnny Coates and his twin brother, Charles, lay in a pile of straw with their younger brother, Zackery. Johnny was expounding his philosophy of life.

"One thing I know for sure is I want to be rich." Johnny looked toward the other boys. They both nodded. Being rich seemed like a damn good thing to be. They already knew all they needed to know about being poor. Talk of being rich was exotic somehow—an unknown foreign land to be happily contemplated.

"Can I be rich with you, Johnny?" Zackery's eyes were a bit too trusting to suit Charles. Charles had heard schemes presented and discarded all his life from the likes of his father, Cyril Coates, and his Uncle Rufus. No doubt, being rich was a good thing, but so far, he had never seen it materialize despite dozens of overheard discussions between the two adults about getting there. Johnny's declaration, along the same vein, seemed an empty extension of that theme. So Charles challenged his brother, as he often did. Of course, challenging his father or uncle would just lead to a whipping. But it was all the more delicious to challenge Johnny because he could do it with impunity.

"How are you going to do that, Johnny?" Charles' dark eyes drilled into Johnny's. "How are you going to get rich?"

"I'm working on that, Brother. I think about it all the time!" Johnny lifted his lips and ran his tongue over his prominent canine teeth. He didn't like being pinned down. He looked at Charles and knew that the intelligence behind those eyes matched his own. They were twins, after all. They were different in some ways but alike in a lot more. The only other kid to challenge him was his older cousin, Elwood. He put up with Elwood primarily because he was bigger, stronger, and had a hot temper if irked. He glanced at Zac, who was taking it in all the while nodding his head. He knew Zac believed in him. He took a lot of satisfaction in that instant approval from little Zac.

A shadow flitted briefly across the mounded hay just before they heard the guttural swearing. The boys' Pa, Cyril Coates, seemed to come at them out of nowhere. He materialized suddenly in the barn's doorway. Spotting them, he staggered forward with the jug of moonshine in his right hand. He tried to unbuckle his belt with his left. His face, already flushed purple from the shine, contorted with rage. The Coates' clan were subsistence share-crop farmers in Travis County, Georgia. Their place was about a hundred miles south of the Tennessee border. Only when pickled and angry, as Cyril was now, did he exhibit this heightened level of vigor.

Today, as usual, the targets for his ire were the twin sons. They were long and lean and healthy. Cyril spent a lot of effort trying to figure out how they could earn their keep. He didn't expect much from their brother, Zackery, yet. The younger boy just followed the two older boys around like a favored dog. As the father staggered through the barn's doorway, Zac quickly crouched down behind a broken wagon wheel leaning against the wall. Early in his young life, he had learned the knack of staying out of his father's line of sight.

"I tole you boys to get them cows out of the north pasture a hour ago!" Cyril couldn't abide disobedience. And he had a favored way to punish it.

"We're going right now, Pa," Charles said. He leaped to his feet, motioned toward Johnny, and made to flee around the angry man's right side and escape through the barn's doorway. His eyes fastened on the belt that his Pa was struggling to pull free. The boys held a deathly fear of the belt, for though it stung less than a switch in the man's hands, it left a deeper welt. Charles' left elbow accidentally struck the jug of shine in his haste, wrenching it from the man's grasp.

"Damnation!" Cyril's eyes followed the jug's trajectory as it hit the packed earth and rolled crazily across the floor, striking a barn post and spinning in a slow arc, leaving a trail of shine in its wake.

The boys' eyes widened. Wasted moonshine would not go unpunished. Desperate, Johnny darted to the left, hoping to evade capture. He knew from experience that in his father's mind, orneriness or disobedience by one of the twins demanded punishment for both. There seemed to be an invisible link between the boys, uniting them into one entity in their father's mind.

The sight of the spinning jug dribbling the precious liquid was enough to focus Cyril's senses. With both hands now free, Cyril abandoned his struggle with the belt for the moment. He reached out his long arms and snared first one boy and then the other around their waists and manhandled them toward the post and dripping jug. "Pick it up!" But instead of allowing time for one of them to obey, he shoved them further ahead of him. His right hand, now free, grasped the belt buckle anew. The length of leather slid free with a light caressing sound as the tip cleared his trousers. Without another word, he brought the thick leather strap right and then left across his body in a looping arc that cracked with sharp reports as six inches of it lashed the flesh of first Charles and then Johnny. The boys brought their arms and hands up to protect their faces as they unsuccessfully jostled each other to put the six-inch width of the post between themselves and their father. Back and forth, the belt lashed them three times in turn. Cyril was panting with the exertion when he bent to retrieve the jug. "Now get your asses out to the north pasture, and don't come back without the cows!"

The boys skedaddled, eager to escape further punishment. Once they cleared the barnyard, Johnny held up and ran his hands up and down his upper arms. He could feel the welts coming up through the fabric of the shirt. "I'm going to kill him!" He looked at Charles, who was rubbing his arms as well. "Someday."

"And you're going to be rich," Charles mocked. A red streak was visible across his shoulder and the back of his neck.

"I ain't lying! I'm going to kill him." Johnny looked back and caught sight of young Zac running to catch up. Charles' eyes followed his. In but a moment, the younger boy joined them.

"Did he whack you too, Zac?" Charles's eyes narrowed.

"Nah, he chased me till I was clear of the barn. Then, he just swore at me about the shine. 'Course you spilled it." Zac drew himself up and was quiet while the older boys continued to massage their wounds.

"Good," Charles said.

"Good." Belatedly, Johnny agreed, though he didn't mean it. It peeved Johnny some every time Zac got off. Cyril had created a pecking order for the three boys. First in line for punishment was Johnny, along with Charles; last was Zac. To Johnny's mind organizing things to suit yourself in that way was one of the significant benefits of being an adult. Adults could do anything they wanted. He was determined to be a grownup someday and do whatever he damn pleased!

"Let's get the cows," Charles said. "I heard Ma and Pa talking this morning. Uncle Rufus done come onto a hog. He said we could come over to his farm this afternoon for shine and barbeque."

"Boy, that will be good," said Zac. He licked his lips in anticipation. Wild game, usually their source of meat, required Cyril to trudge through the woods. Of late, Cyril had found that unappealing. So it was always exciting when one of the adults came onto an opportunity to steal something tasty.

"Except Uncle Rufus is as ready to give me a licking as Pa," Johnny said.

"Yeah, and he uses that crop on his boys," Charles said.

"And me," Johnny remembered his last encounter with the liquored-up little man. "I'll kill him someday, too," Johnny said the words under his breath. He rubbed his sore arms some more.

The upside of visiting Uncle Rufus, aside from the pork, was that he and Charles and the six oldest cousins could come upon some of the moonshine once the men passed out. Uncle Rufus did make some powerful shine!

After the agitation in the barn, the walk to the north forty for the cows was a pleasant journey. Charles was the practical twin. He put the beating behind him as best the pain of his injuries allowed. Johnny's mind, as always, grasped unsuccessfully at a hundred ways to gain revenge. He rubbed his injured arms and pictured the day he was big enough to challenge his Pa directly. He walked a bit apart from Charles and Zac. In his ire, he considered the tumbled-down out-buildings and the decaying fences. He agreed with Rufus and Cyril that fixing fences seemed like a waste of time, for there was no money in it. One of the things Johnny had come to understand from his adult kinfolk was the value of making a quick dollar. He had heard that expression all his life. Both men's mantra was "a quick dollar." Whenever a job presented itself, the first question was always, would it result in "a quick dollar"? If the answer was no, the proposal was abandoned. Then one of the men would pull out the jug to drown the issue in moonshine.

Johnny grasped the fact that most quick dollars were the result of "coming onto" things. Most people called it thieving. And for young and old members of the Coates Clan, a quick dollar didn't refer to just money. A pie left in a windowsill; a couple of tomatoes dropped into a coat pocket; a doodad swiped at the general store were minor forms of quickly coming onto things. Sly visits to the stores during the busiest part of the day, finding something valuable and slipping away before the merchant even knew that they had been there, was a crowning achievement of coming onto things.

Johnny's stomach rumbled in anticipation of the barbeque.

The family acknowledged Uncle Rufus as the success story of the clan. He had developed a good business selling his moonshine. Sales to neighbors and trades with merchants for other commodities lifted his family to a slightly higher standard than enjoyed by his close kin. Uncle Rufus's idea of luxury was a plug of tobacco. The man's notion of success influenced the boys in ways not intended. They all learned to take advantage of the adult's inattention to come onto a chaw or a drink as often as possible.

Soon the four cows were rounded up and headed toward the barn. Two had been come onto over in Jones County as calves the year before. Cyril hid any stray or stolen animals he happened to come onto in the back forty until they matured enough to be unrecognizable or could be slaughtered for the table. Cyril and Rufus lived by only one rule, never steal from their immediate neighbors or relatives of their close neighbors. It was a bedrock rule until Rufus decided to break it.

The idea of making an exception developed that afternoon at the barbeque. Rufus was the oldest of the two brothers. His supremacy within the family was assured because he had the oldest son and had sired four boys, whereas Cyril was short one son with only three. Rufus's older sister, Jane, and her husband, Evert, also had only three sons. Though the smallest of the three men, Rufus made up in swagger what he lacked in size. To his mind putting on a barbeque for three families was a powerful confirmation of his position as the clan's leader. But today, because his near neighbor, Ronald Dawson, had disparaged the quality of Rufus's last batch of shine, the little man was out of sorts. He took pride in his moonshine. He was so prideful that he had even endeavored to teach his oldest son, Schooley, his secret recipe and distilling methods beyond the basic manual labor required to prepare the ingredients. The boy seemed to catch on quickly, leading Rufus to declare to the rest of the family that the boy was the brightest youngster in the county.

Rufus broached the subject with Cyril after everyone had eaten their fill, and the older boys had run off to pitch horseshoes. "I sure would like to fix that Dawson good."

"Why's that?" His brother-in-law, Evert, lifted the jug and took a double swig. He was a big man, and he reckoned he needed a double swig.

Cyril just looked on. He was already getting a little glassy-eyed. He knew his older brother well enough to know he had contemplated an idea for a bit before bringing up the subject.

"Never you mind why!" Rufus reached for the jug, and Evert passed it over with a nod. He was a large man of little curiosity but could be set off like gunpowder if he felt belittled. Evert kept a tight rein on his mousy wife and household but with less fanfare than the two brothers. He had only asked the question to be polite to the host. If Rufus didn't want to talk about it, it was okay with him.

Rufus looked at Cyril and pursed his lips. The words had slipped out due to the shine. There was no reason to involve an outsider like his brother-in-law. He would discuss it privately with Cyril later. Rufus took another swig. The barbeque and corn whisky were settling happily in his stomach. Finally, he felt himself dozing off. He glanced around and realized that the other two men's eyes had already closed. A quick nap was a pleasant way to finish off the afternoon. Evert would take Jane and their kids home before dark. Rufus's wife, Margaret, and Cyril's Nancy would throw down pallets for the kids and spend the night. He'd talk with Cyril then. Being in charge felt real good! He inhaled one more measure of fumes from the jug and shoved the cork home before he dozed off.

The men napped for a little while before any of the boys pitching horseshoes noticed. When Johnny noted that the men were asleep, he edged up slowly and came onto the jug. He shook it a little and found it over half full. An empty jug lay sideways on the ground. Johnny ran toward the barn, and the other boys hightailed after him. He took a generous swig and felt the heat reignite the barbeque in his stomach. He handed the jug to big Elwood, who chugged some. Next, it went to Charles, who tasted a little, and passed it on to the oldest cousin, Schooley. By the time the container had passed around to all eight of the older boys, there were barely fumes for the two younger ones. They got but a drop or so each. Johnny made sure they didn't leave any by turning the jug upside down and breathing deep while he waited for the last drop. Finally, it hung on the rim, and he licked it off. He pushed the cork back in and handed the jug to Zac. "Now, take this back real quiet and leave it by Uncle Rufus. That way, he'll think he got the last swig."

Zac did as told. When he returned, he found all the boys laid up in the hay. Their eyes were already closed. He lay down near cousin Barney, and the two youngest cousins were soon asleep as well.

An angry argument awoke the boys an hour later. Johnny and Charles were the first to raise their heads. Rufus and Cyril were having at it up by the house.

"That is the stupidest thing you have ever come up with, Rufus." Cyril's wrath pushed past the myth that Rufus was the unquestioned leader. He stood over the smaller man with his giant balled fists resting on his hips. "You don't steal from your near neighbors!"

"I know that!" Rufus yelled back. With Evert deep asleep, he had decided to broach his idea earlier than he had planned. "Usually, you don't, but that snake made fun of my shine, and I'm not going to let him get away with it!" He glanced toward the boys who first ran into hearing range of the argument, then edged up more slowly as they got close.

"Who gives a shit what Ronald Dawson thinks about anything?" Cyril shook his head at the stupidity of the argument.

"Listen, Cyril. If Dawson goes around badmouthing my shine, the next thing you know, my business goes to pieces," Rufus stamped his foot. "I won't put up with it!"

"Well, what you're planning won't keep him from doing that, will it?" Cyril responded.

"No, but making a lot of shine with free corn will save me a heap of money to make up for the lost business." Rufus made a face meant to emphasize his cunning. He tapped his finger against his temple. "See, Cyril, you just aren't thinking this through." The little man's smile lit up his face. Johnny turned toward Charles and rolled his eyes. He could tell that Rufus had invented this particular argument on the fly and now pretended to have already worked it out.

"This old worn-out farm don't produce enough corn for my mash," he continued. "I have to buy it. I need the rest of the land for cotton. There ain't much of that either." Rufus noticed the boys approach and turned his back to take a few steps away. Cyril glanced around and followed along. The old saying, "little pitchers have big ears," was well known by both men.

Johnny ran his hands up and down his sore arms testing out the welts. The brutal ridges of flesh were easy to locate with his fingertips. Again, Johnny felt a stab of disdain for his Pa. The man didn't have a quick comeback. Johnny ran his tongue over his prominent canines and looked at Charles. The other boy was kicking with his toe at a half-buried rock. Johnny wondered if Charles was thinking the same thing he was.

"Alright, alright, forget it." Rufus spat. He headed for the shed, where he made his shine to get another jug. The boys' eyes met. They were both shocked by Rufus's capitulation. That's when Johnny came up with his plan.

It was well after dark when the two brothers snuck out to the barn to harness the horses. By the time they rode half a mile to the Dawson farm, they could barely see. They waited in the trees until the sole light near the farmhouse window went dark. They waited another half hour before approaching. There were separate lanes from the road to the house and the barn. A fancy picket fence surrounded the house. The only sound as they hitched the horses to the wagon was the nickering between those in the barn and their own. After a few minutes, the wagon lurched forward through the gate. There was still no life from the house.

Johnny looked over in the darkness. He could see Charles twisted around to stare toward the farmhouse. He remembered Charles' litany of questions.

"What will we do if Mister Dawson runs out on his porch with a shotgun? What will we do if he has dogs we didn't know about? What will we do when they catch us in the road with a wagon of stolen corn?" Johnny could feel the beads of sweat sliding down his temples. Johnny had pushed all of Charles's questions aside at the beginning of this little adventure. Now the adrenaline was running strong. He loved the feeling of an adventure! He loved using his fast-talking enthusiasm to flummox his brother. He loved the sense of superiority for doing something his Pa and his uncle didn't have the guts to do. That was what it came down to, guts. He had guts, and they didn't!

"It'll be easy," he had told Charles as they discussed the plan. "We'll ride the team over to Dawson's place at dusk. We'll wait till dark. Then, hook up our horses to his wagon and haul a whole load of corn back here."

"No," Charles had said flatly.

"It'll be so dark no one will see us. It's a short run. We won't be on the road for ten minutes. We'll come into Uncle Rufus' property by the back gate. We'll unload the corn on the backside of the barn. Won't he be surprised come morning!" John ignored Charles' protests. He knew he could carry his brother along on zeal, just like Rufus often did with their father.

"How do you know there's a wagon full of corn?" Charles had looked at Johnny suspiciously.

"I saw it when we passed by, coming here," Johnny said impatiently. "It makes sense. It's Friday. He's probably planning to take it to town in the morning to sell."

The plan worked just like Johnny said. No dogs barked. Dawson didn't run out with a shotgun. They met no one on the darkened road. When they reached the back of Rufus' barn, they removed the tailgate. Half of the ears of corn slid out of their own accord. The boys lay down in the bed and used their legs and feet to push out the rest. Everything went according to plan. Johnny felt jubilation at the success. He just wished that everyone in Travis County could know! But despite his outward scorn, there was the knowledge that come morning, the two most important men in his life would know! This success would show Rufus and Cyril that he wasn't worthless!

They drove the empty wagon back to the road. But as the boys ascended the roadside of the bar ditch, Johnny had another idea.

"I know! We'll drive the wagon back to Dawson's place and leave it! But, boy, I'd like to see the look on his face when he comes out tomorrow morning!"

"No!" Charles said.

"It will be perfect!"

"No!" Charles said again. He leaped from the wagon and walked back toward the barn. Johnny watched him for a minute and weighed his options. It was obvious that Charlie was jealous at the success. It was for sure more dangerous to take the wagon back to Dawson's farm. But it would be more fun. But there would be nobody to share these further heroics with now that Charles was gone. That was the deciding factor. Nobody could ever know, except Rufus and Cyril. Now, Johnny dismissed them with disdain, for they didn't have any guts! He turned right to take the wagon further down the road as he had initially planned. Who gave a shit if he impressed those two?

Early the following day, Ronald Dawson and Sheriff Hopkins rode up the short lane to Rufus' door before the sun cleared the distant eastern hills. Rufus was hitching up his suspenders as he came out of the outhouse. His eyes grew large at the sight of the lawman. His mind searched his recent history, trying to think of a reason for the visit. There were several possibilities, but the stolen pig he had come onto the previous week and shared with the family the day before could be the primary suspect though it hadn't belonged to Dawson. He was confident of that story. He had mulled it over in his mind several times. He was about to offer the Sheriff his hand when the lawman said the words that threw him for a loop.

"Where'd you get that corn piled up outside your barn, Rufus?"

"What?" He stared up at the man's star and felt his ire rise. "What corn?"

"You're saying you don't have a pile of corn behind your barn?" The Sheriff glanced over at Dawson and back. "We can see it from the road, Rufus!"

"You can? There is?" Rufus shook his head in confusion. Was he having a dream? Was he still lying up in his bed? Rufus almost felt around on himself to verify his wakefulness. "Sheriff, I don't know what you're talking about!"

The commotion drew the rest of the clan out on the porch. Cyril and Nancy looked at the scene and each other. Cyril had shared Rufus's aborted plan with his wife after they went to bed the previous night. The conversation was puzzling. Cyril was doubly perplexed. The man hadn't followed through, after all, had he? Nothing made any sense. Nancy put her hand on Zackery's shoulder and looked around for her other boys. She found them standing behind her, staring wide-eyed at the sheriff's badge.

"Johnny, Charles?" She stepped to the side and turned to face them.

The boys looked at each other and prepared to make a break, but Cyril came alert. He grabbed them by their shirt collars. He turned back toward the Sheriff and spoke up. The quicker the sheriff could be dispatched from the farm, the better.

"I think I know what happened, Sheriff." He glared at Rufus. "These boys got the idea that Rufus needed corn, and they decided to help out." His face was red as the anger churned up. His grasp of the boy's shoulders tightened, heavy and dangerous.

"I bet it was that chickenshit, Johnny." Rufus fumed.

"It was not!" Johnny wrenched around and pointed at Charles. "It was Charles' idea. I just helped!"

Charles shot his brother a look that would have scalded a cat. Johnny's denial and finger-pointing were the worst kind of betrayal.

Rufus started for the porch. He began to mount the steps. His hands were unbuckling his belt. "I'll deal with you, you little snot-nosed kid." Cyril pushed him back so roughly that he stumbled and almost fell.

"I'll take care of this." Cyril jerked the two boys down the steps and pushed them to face forward against the side of the house. Charles heard the whisper of the leather as the belt cleared Cyril's trousers. He received three lashes. Johnny got two. This time there was no post to absorb part of the blows. Both boys had fallen to their knees, faces pressed against the side of the house when Cyril spoke again. "You never do nothing unless I tell you to." He popped the belt again and gave Charles an extra swat. "Do you understand?" There was silence. He drew his arm back, preparing another blow.

"Yes, Pa," Charles spoke through clenched teeth. The big man's hand hesitated, then fell to his side. Charles looked sidewise at Johnny. His eyes, through a few tears, were sharp. His lips trembled just a little, but his voice was unmistakable. "Yes, Pa," he said again.

Rufus Coates looked up innocently at the mounted lawman. Gaining the attention of the law was no small thing. He would have really laid into the boys personally given a chance.

"I'm right sorry, Sheriff. I guess the boys thought it would be fun to pull a prank on Mister Dawson," Rufus said. "Cyril and me didn't know nothing about it. But, sir, if you'll bring your wagon over, we'll get it loaded for you before you know it." Rufus said as he turned toward his neighbor. He stopped and stared at Dawson's expression. The man was strangely ashenfaced from watching the display of Coates' discipline.

"Okay," was the only word Dawson could manage. He suddenly reined his horse around and headed for the road. The sheriff nodded and followed close behind.

Rufus was itching to get his own hands on the boys, but Cyril was disinclined to cooperate. Cyril knew where the blame for the idea of the corn theft belonged. But his greatest ire was still toward the two boys. It was one thing to steal; it was a mortal sin to get caught.

Dawson brought the wagon over and loaded the corn. Then he drove it east toward town. Once the work was complete, all but one of the boys trooped toward the house for breakfast. If anyone had looked down the road in the opposite direction in the wake of the wagon's departure, they would have seen the slight fourteen-year-old Charles walking toward the western horizon. Charles Coats limped a little from the welts on his legs as he walked down the lonely road. He had no plan or destination. It wasn't the poverty or the meanness or the pain of whippings that settled his mind to escape his family forever. Those were things he could tolerate. But the two extra stinging welts on the back of his legs were reminders of the deep betrayal by the boy he called brother and left Charles with no other answer.

Johnny did notice. When he spotted his brother, he realized what was happening, and the corners of his mouth turned down in a smirk. Good riddance! Charles had always been a pain in the ass. Johnny gave no thought to his betrayal of his brother, or of raising the alarm at his departure. By blaming Charles, he had cleverly evaded two lashes with the belt! Johnny silently examined his new injuries and remembered the triumphant thrill of his brief success stealing the corn. His only other serious antagonist was his older, equally worthless cousin, Elwood. Maybe someday he'd see that he got his comeuppance too! But first he'd make Cyril pay.

THE END

Cal Jordon, CALL TO ARMS

Cal Jordon's broad forehead wrinkled in concentration. His spine stiffened as he scanned the Titustown newspaper's first page. The bold headline proclaimed victory for the Confederacy at Chickamauga, Tennessee. Of course, he had already heard the news, but seeing it in the newspaper seemed to make it official. Since Harlon County was only an eight-hour march from that battlefield, he could breathe a long sigh of relief. He searched the news story for more details.

Loud voices turned his attention toward the front of the Lucky Star Tavern for a moment, where a few of his elderly neighbors were celebrating the Confederate win.

"I told you them Union boys couldn't fight! Oh, they got better equipment and more troops, but when the chips are down, our southern boys will lick them almost every time," Ed Thomas proclaimed.

"Them Yankees got their tails whipped for sure," Bill Simmons chimed in.

Cal glanced back down at the casualty numbers and frowned. It seemed to him that although the Confederates stopped the Yankees' advance, the Yankees had done pretty well for themselves. Their estimated losses included sixteen hundred dead. The Rebels had lost two thousand three hundred dead, and more Confederate boys were wounded than Yankees. The only positive number was the reported captured or missing with three times as many Yankees as Rebels. But, he reminded himself again, their progress south had been halted. That was a critical fact.

He stood, slapped his hat on his head, and folded the paper. Cal's farm was closer to this particular battlefield than was comfortable for him to think about. A win by the North could have resulted in the Yankees overrunning the county. He had heard it was common for Yankee troops to loot and burn. Everything he and his neighbors had worked so hard for could very well have been destroyed. So, Cal and everyone else roundabout had very personal reasons for feeling relief for the victory.

Just as concerning was the itch by his twenty-year-old son, Jimmy, to take off with his friends to defend the honor of the South. So far, Cal had successfully tamped down that dangerous impulse. He hoped he could use the latest victory to bolster his contention that the South had things under control. Early on, Cal had been pleased when the governor had stood up against Jefferson Davis' call to pull men out of Georgia to join army units in other states. That need for troops was a bottomless pit.

Some of the early volunteers were already back. Too many of them had returned in a box. More came back with wounds both physical and mental that would never heal.

From Cal's perspective, war, any war, was to be avoided. But, of course, if Yankees showed up in Harlon County, he'd strap on his gun just like everyone else. He thought about Pappy Jordon. His feisty uncle had come back from the Mexican War in eighteen forty-seven, a bit changed from when he'd left. The difference was subtle. He was still a gutsy little man, but those who knew him best could sense something. There was a sad bitterness beneath the sass. And then there was old Captain Fred Ingerstall, who led a company of volunteers west to Texas and returned with his only son's remains. Old Fred had died years later, leaving no heirs to one of the better valley farms.

The men at the table looked up as Cal headed for the door.

"You saw the paper, Cal." One of the men grabbed his elbow as Cal passed. "We been telling you things are going to turn for us!" The other men's heads were bobbing in agreement. Cal could tell that they were genuinely enthused.

Cal smiled and responded sarcastically. "I guess we can keep our slaves now, can't we, Burl?"

"You bet we can!" Burl's smile diminished a little, but he let the comment pass. Neither he nor any of the other men in the Star owned any slaves. Farming the valleys and foothills in northwest Georgia, it was unlikely they ever would. None of the men chewing the fat in the tavern were like Fred Ingerstall, who had brought two field hands and a couple of house servants with him from the Georgia coast. When Fred's most trusted black man, old Isiah, died a few years later, Fred had chosen not to replace him.

Though slavery was a big part of it, it wasn't just the right to own slaves that stirred the emotions of many of Cal's neighbors.

It was the notion that the northern states deemed themselves so superior. Cal wondered if a New Yorker or a Chicagoan would have the same attitude about slavery if they depended on them as much as the South did or at least thought it did. Cal wasn't blind to the fact that commercial interests often taint the definitions of right and wrong.

Yankee was a dirty word to most southerners, even for those who would never own a slave. Despite early Rebel optimism, invading Yankee soldiers had turned out to be devilishly good shots. The consensus was that every Yankee deserved shooting. The latest battle tended to raise expectations again. It was a nasty business, and General Lee's recruiters were making ever more frequent visits to Harlon County looking for more men.

That evening, Cal, his wife Wanda, Jimmy, and the two little girls, Lilly and Gladys, encircled the big oak table chatting about frivolous things when Jimmy brought up his bombshell news.

"Pa, I've got two announcements to make," Jimmy grinned at his parents. His Mother lay her fork back on her plate. She was suddenly ashen-faced. She and Cal had discussed the dark prospect of Jimmy entering military service. Jimmy's two young sisters looked at their older brother expectantly. Jimmy's grin and this interruption of the conversation hinted at a surprise, and they loved surprises!

For a long moment, Cal stared at his wife and then began to chew again. He was afraid to look at his son. Cal just knew that his premonition after reading the newspaper was coming true. Cal's mind churned for something, anything, that he could say to move things beyond the next few minutes. But then his mind latched on the word "two." Had Jimmy said he had two things?

He took a breath. Maybe his boy wasn't going to put on a uniform after all? Perhaps he would talk about two funny things or two dumb things or two exciting things? "Two things!" Cal felt his heart settle back into its rhythmic beating once again. Then, he realized that Jimmy was staring at him with an expectant expression on his face. He was waiting for him to respond. Wanda and the two little girls' eyes had also fastened on Cal.

"Well, son, what's your news?" Cal forced a smile despite his initial concerns and took a deep breath.

"Well, first, I asked Sarah Tyson to marry me!" Jimmy's face lit up like the sun rising over Homestead Mountain.

Cal looked at Wanda to confirm that she was as stunned as he was. Her mouth was open as she looked at her son.

"How did this come about?" Baffled, Cal scrutinized his son. He knew the boy was captivated by the pretty girl. But he had no idea they were anywhere close to marriage!

"Well," Jimmy leaned forward and put his elbows on the table. "Well, first I heard that George Masters asked her to marry him, and Sarah said no. Then Billy Roy asked, and she said no again. I knew she really liked George. I could see her turning down Bobby Roy, but I'd have guessed that it would be George if she'd say yes to anyone."

"I don't understand," Wanda said. "You asked her to marry you because she turned down two other boys?" She squinted her eyes as if it would help her follow the logic.

"What's the hurry, Son?" Cal was in over his depth. Eighteen-year-old Sarah was a fine girl. Miss Emmy's niece worked with her aunt, who owned the Lucky Star Hotel and Tavern. She was easily the prettiest girl in town. She was intelligent and resourceful, it seemed. But no matter how much Cal rolled it around in his head, he couldn't make sense of it.

"Why the big rush to get married?" Cal felt the dread building again.

"Well, that's the second thing. Bobby Roy, George Master, Joe Johnson, and I have signed up to join the Army of the Confederacy! We just heard that our boys won at Chickamauga! The recruiter says that if we pour it on now, we'll run them Yankees all the way back to where they came from!"

There was a collective hush around the table. Even Gladys and Lilly grasped the consequences of the last announcement. Jimmy would be going away, and he might be gone a long time. He could get badly hurt, or he might not come back at all!

"No!" Cal stood and stared down at his son. "That's crazy! We," he looked at Wanda. "We didn't feed and clothe you for twenty years to have you go off and get yourself shot!" The import of that last word pulled all of the strength out of his legs. It felt like he was jinxing the boy. He sat down hard and put his hand to his forehead as if to compose himself.

"Pa, my friends are all going! My best friends are going. I can't sit here and let them go alone!" Jimmy had heard enough from his father over the last year to know where the man stood on the War. Jimmy also knew that everyone said his great uncle, Pappy Jordon, was a Mexican War hero. The fact that Pappy wouldn't talk about his experiences while he was in Texas only added luster to his heroism. Jimmy knew that something terrible must have happened. Aside from the fact that old man Ingerstall had come back with his dead son, he didn't know any details.

Jimmy had always respected Uncle Pappy. Folks said he was a hero. Wasn't that a good thing?

"Pa? Uncle Pappy saved the lives of seven men. If he hadn't gone, those men probably would have died. If Bobby and George and Joe don't come back, I'll never forgive myself. What if I could have saved them?"

Cal felt the noose of Jimmy's argument tighten around his throat. He could think of no rebuttal. How could you teach a boy to be responsible, protect the good, and fight evil in the world and argue the opposite when he thought he was acting in accordance with his training? Cal wondered with a sinking heart if he had forgotten to teach his son something just as important. That there is gray as well as black and white. That "good" is not a word that stands on its own. That it is propped up and sustained by the circumstances in which men apply it. Looking at Jimmy's earnest expression, Cal doubted himself as a father. It was a painful condemnation. He looked at Wanda. Would she question him now for his failure? No, there was no contempt contained in her expression. There was alarm. There was sadness, but it was a misery that would still let him in.

Cal looked back at his son and sighed. He did not have the heart to argue further. To do so would appear to renounce all that he had taught the boy. Moreover, it could break the bond of trust between them that Cal had spent half his life nurturing. Cal dropped his head to his chest for a moment and closed his mind against the fear. He searched for something, anything, positive in the situation. The boy was going to marry the prettiest girl in Harlon County, after all. That was something to celebrate.

Surely the Almighty would bring Jimmy back to her if not to his loving family.

"When's this wedding going to happen, Son?" Cal smiled a little and felt the release of tension around the table. Lilly and Gladys cried out in joy.

"Maybe we can be brides' maids?" Lilly clasped her hands together.

Jimmy grinned. "Well, I'm not sure you're old enough. Are you old enough?"

"Yes!" the girls cried in chorus. "But, Mother, don't we need special dresses?" Lilly grabbed her mother's hand.

"We all leave the first of October," Jimmy said. "So, it will have to be soon. I guess Sarah and Miss Emmy will work that out?"

"I'll visit with them about it at church Sunday." Wanda wiped her eyes with her napkin. Cal doubted that the tears were of happiness. He felt empty now, for he was sure of only one thing. Watching his boy go off to war would be the hardest thing he would ever have to do.

THE END

Preacher, HONOR BUT NO GLORY

Alabama, 1865. Twenty-one-year-old Bill, "Bronco" Brumley, was lying on his belly with his prized Henry rifle tucked close to his side. He was a lean young man with dark curly hair spilling out from under his blue Union cap. A hint of a mustache curved across his upper lip. In his brief military career, Bronco had faced enemy fire often enough to stifle any eagerness to jump up and charge through the mire that surrounded him. His squad had reentered this skirmish area just before first light. He peered nervously right and left for a hint of their next move. Up until now, every offensive effort had bogged down. It seemed that the valley between the steep jack-oak-covered hills was the home of every kind of bramble known to man.

Finally, through the early morning mist, he caught sight of another blue uniform fifteen paces away to his right. His weathered face registered relief, then astonishment as he realized that it was not someone he recognized. *Dang, what happened to my squad?* His squad was part of an infantry company assigned to clean out Rebels' nests in Limestone and Madison counties in northern Alabama. The vegetation was fed by a slow-moving trickle of water over algae-covered rocks, making the footing tricky. The Confederate soldiers at the other end of the draw had the advantage of being well barricaded. Their intermittent rifle fire whistled through the underbrush. The hornets were ample warning to the Union men hunkered down in the wet. Both sides were trying unsuccessfully to gain some momentum.

Bronco closed his eyes, ruminating for a moment, a half-smile forming on his chapped lips. In Bronco's mind's eye, he was back in Ohio slipping off a wild stallion that no one else had been able to ride. His boss, old Sam Jacobs, was slapping him on the back, calling him "Bronco Brumley." After breaking a few more difficult broncs, the nickname stuck.

A round kicked up dirt ten feet to his left. Bronco's head jerked up, and he wondered if he had momentarily fallen asleep. He looked around to reorient himself. The blue-clad figure to his right was gone. *Tarnation!* He crept right. *Don't panic!* The lump in the pit of his stomach was growing by the minute. *Maybe if he went to that man's last position, he could follow his trail?*

He crawled to the right. A barely perceptible breeze thinned the mist for a moment, and now he could see a bit better. Three blue uniforms were hunched down in the brush a few feet apart, about sixty feet directly ahead of him. The Rebels fired another ragged volley. He ducked as a couple of hornets whistled through the nearby undergrowth. Bronco looked up just in time to see one of the three men in front cry out and topple sideways. The other two men flattened out deeper in the leaves and dead bush. "Hunkered down like ticks on a hound dog," Bronco muttered to himself.

He knew he had best follow their example and keep low. So, propelling himself with his elbows, he slithered over the rough ground toward the three.

Bronco heard the shortest of the men, a barrel-chested corporal stage whisper to his companion as he approached. "The Lieutenant's down, Sarge!"

Bronco scrambled over the remaining few feet and sprawled alongside the corporal, who he did not recognize. He could see a young man with a Lieutenant's bar on his shoulder lying with both of his hands clutching himself at the beltline. The officer spoke through gritted white teeth and lips, taut with pain.

"Dammit!" The lieutenant's eyes darted around as if searching for something or someone who could undo the wound in his belly. Then, finally, they settled on the corporal. "Dammit, Preacher, I'm gut shot!"

The thickset corporal pulled off his cap to lean in and peer closer at the lieutenant's midsection, and then he twisted toward the new arrival with surprise. The shape of his big head reminded Bronco of a four-cornered anvil. He had wide-spaced teeth set in a lantern jaw. He had not shaved for several days. His gray eyes narrowed as he realized that Bronco was a stranger to him. "Who?"

"Private Brumley, Corporal. 'B' Company."

"Help me get this coat out of the way, Private."

Blood was already forming around the bullet's entry point. Bronco recoiled at the notion of putting his hands in the bloody mess but did as ordered. He lay his rifle down and unbuttoned the debris-laden coat. He pulled the jacket open and spread it aside, revealing the scarlet liquid. The lieutenant moved his hands to touch the spot. Bronco pushed the hands a bit to the side and loosened the belt buckle. A groove across it traced a mini ball's path before penetrating the softer adjacent flesh. The lieutenant's eyes took in Bronco without recognition, and he let his hands slide limply to his sides. More blood was slowly puddling against the waistband. The husky corporal experimentally stuck his little finger about half an inch into the wound.

"I can feel the pill, Sir." He stage-whispered. "I don't think it made it through to your gut."

The third man, a tall sergeant, had acted as a sentinel until now. He rose to his knees for a moment, took aim at a place below where powder smoke was rising, and fired into the brush. His aim was good, and they heard a cry as the sergeant swung back toward them and dropped to his knees. He was a decade younger than the Corporal with flint-hard eyes set over a straight nose and taut lips. His uniform, like theirs, was caked with rotting matter from rolling around on the ground. He elbowed closer and quickly scanned Lieutenant Adams' beltline for himself.

"I hope you're right," he said. Then his eyes traveled down the Lieutenant's body. "Preacher!" he motioned. Redirecting their gaze, they could see that the injured man's left leg bent unnaturally. Blood was also seeping through the lieutenant's pants.

"Shoot." Preacher bent closer and eyed the second wound.

Lieutenant Adams lifted his head a few inches, and his eyes tried to follow Preacher's gaze. "I can't feel a thing down there."

"The knee looks shattered, Sir," the sergeant said. The pace of the gunfire increased. Now, between the ragged volleys, they heard the far-off thrashing of men edging their way through the brush. The Rebels were coming closer. "Sarge, they're making their play. It sounds like they have reinforcements." Preacher said.

The sergeant peered through the bramble and put his face close to the lieutenant. "We have to get you out of here, Sir." He reached down and grasped the tattered fabric surrounding the knee on two sides and ripped it the rest of the way around. He worked the torn strip to fashion a crude tourniquet that he double knotted.

The lieutenant focused on Bronco for the first time.

"Fall back, soldier." The eyes seemed a little out of focus. Lieutenant Adam's legs started shaking as shock began to set in. "Jones, you and Preacher fall back too." The officer twisted around to access his holstered pistol.

"Hand me my rifle," he said.

"Sir, we aren't leaving you." Sergeant Jones's expression was grim.

"I can't walk or crawl. I'll cover you as long as I can."

"No, sir," Sarge said.

Preacher forced a grin and ended the discussion. "Let's save the chit-chat for later. So what say, we all find a quieter place, Sarge." He leaned in close and matter-of-factly removed the pistol from the lieutenant's shaking hand. He tucked it in his belt. Preacher drew up his muscular legs to gather himself in the lull of rifle fire, then thrust with the thick stumps to heave himself to his feet. He grabbed the lieutenant's right arm with a grunt of determination, drew the man up, and clumsily fitted him across his shoulder. He and Sarge exchanged a glance.

"Let's get the hell out of here," Sarge whispered.

Bronco was up in an instant. He slip-slid close on their heels as they picked their way among the many tracks. Having his back to the enemy sent a shiver through Bronco. The surest course was to follow the direction of the trickle of water. It was the only consistent landmark in the shifting fog.

A row of massive boulders forced them to navigate toward the creek's center, where there was less cover. Hornets came flying.

"Keep going, Preacher! We'll cover you," Sarge ordered.

Preacher did not respond other than to slog ahead. Sarge threw himself behind one of the boulders, intent on keeping the Rebel's heads down. Bronco, torn between joining him or following Preacher, followed suit. Looking back, they could barely see the outlines of three men in gray, still a good way off but relentlessly moving forward. One of the men raised his rifle, indicating he spotted a target.

Lord, get me out of here. Sarge and Bronco fired at the man together, and the Rebel went down. Bronco breathed when the remaining Rebels fired back.

One of the incoming rounds zipped past Bronco like a dragonfly. The round hit the boulder at an angle and threw a spray of rock chips and sand into Sarge's face and peppered the back of Bronco's neck. They both swore in surprise and pain.

"Damnit, I can't see." Sarge dabbed wildly at his cheeks and eyes. He set his rifle down and tried to clear his vision. Bronco ran his hand over the back of his neck and swiped away grit and a little blood. The sergeant was still helplessly trying to clear his vision.

"There's no time for that!" Bronco grabbed Sarge's left wrist and guided his hand to the tail of his coat. "Grab on, Sergeant." He picked up the man's rifle as a hornet passed nearby, and another Rebel stumbled into view. As they made their way forward, the obstacle-strewn trail seemed obstructed at every turn. Bronco slipped and fell, regained his feet, and fell again. Sarge cried out in frustration but hung on, sometimes stumbling, pulling Bronco down, sometimes blindly helping Bronco to his feet while flailing at the steady stream of tears and tenacious grit obstructing his vision.

Twice more, they stopped to catch their wind. Each time, Bronco and Sarge abandoned their positions under fire. Never had Bronco been so desperate. With Sarge blinded, everything depended on him. That assignment pushed him to the limit of his endurance. One more step. One more rock. Another step.

"Hang on, Sergeant." Bronco encouraged Sarge, and when he was almost at the end of his rope, Sarge, even in his blindness, helped him. In his brief life, Bronco had never before felt such responsibility. As they moved toward their presumed haven, Sarge couldn't restrain himself from trying to clear his eyes.

A hundred yards ahead of Sarge and Bronco, Preacher stumbled forward. He skirted around some large boulders and stepped down awkwardly on an algae-covered rock. He slipped sidewise and felt his human burden shift briefly out of his control. As the blood from the lieutenant's stomach wound accumulated, Preacher lost the benefit of friction to hold the man in place. He was keenly aware that the lieutenant could as likely die from striking his head on the rocks as from his wounds if he fell.

Preacher tried to estimate how far they were from camp. He had long ago learned the value of distraction. He turned his mind inward. His work on his father's farm and farrier shop made him robust and tenacious. His ongoing conflicts with his classmate, Billy Barns, taught him toughness and self-awareness. Preacher carefully stepped around a log as he remembered one of their grade school conflicts that led to the blows that landed them in the headmaster's office. Each told their version of events. After the excuses and stories were over, Mister Ingram, the headmaster, nodded and looked keenly at the stocky young man.

"Robert, I have considered you to be a peaceable man." He frowned. "Will you continue to be a peaceable man?" The boy nodded. He realized that it was a good evaluation of his nature. Given the choice of running or fighting, he would fight. Years later, he and Billy eventually settled their scores. Preacher's thoughts returned to the present. Dodging around a hole, he wondered what Billy Barnes was doing just now? Was he bogged down in some hellish battlefield as well?

Preacher stopped to rest with a hand on his knee and then adjusted his load. The lieutenant's blood had soaked both of his shoulders by now. Preacher was vividly aware that just one hornet could finish not only him but the young man he carried as well. He trudged forward, across some loose dry rocks that shifted under his feet but were more predictable than the green algae.

Preacher's musings were the distractions he needed to ignore the pain in his knees, his exhaustion, and to avoid thinking about his most pressing concern; maybe the lieutenant was already dead.

Just then, Preacher was relieved to feel lieutenant Adams stiffen a bit, and his thoughts returned to his present dilemma. He was thankful for the assurance that the lieutenant was still alive. He leaned the young officer one-legged against one of the boulders. Preacher pulled a canteen from his shoulder and offered the man water. He watched while Adams lifted both of his hands weakly to drink. The trembling fingers allowed the water to leak around his lips. Both men froze at the sound of a foreign voice.

"You boys don't move a muscle!" The gruff southern accent interrupted their use of the canteen. Preacher turned. The man had a shotgun pointed equal distance between the two men. He looked more like a mountain man than a soldier. Only his gray Rebel cap declared his allegiance. "One of you Yankees killed my brother a while ago. Now I'm going to blast you to kingdom come." He seemed to savor the moment. Preacher searched the man's face. The eyes smoldered with vengeance. "I want you boys to know that you're paying the price for killing a good boy. I had to watch him die." He looked at the blood-soaked Lieutenant Adams. "Looks like I got here too late for him." He swung the gun an inch to the right to center the barrel on Preacher. He pressed his lips together, and Preacher saw him brace to fire. In the moment of preparation, there was the crack of a rifle to the Rebel's rear. The man made a feeble motion toward his neck and pitched forward. Blood spurted from his throat as he fell. He was dead in an instant. Bronco Brumley appeared out of the mist. Preacher suddenly felt too weak to stand. He slumped against the Lieutenant.

"Dang, that was close!" Bronco said as he hurried up with Sarge, who was still grasping his coattail.

"What happened?" Sarge fanned at his tear-flooded eyes.

"A loose Rebel," Bronco said.

Preacher could see that Sarge was in pain. He looked at Bronco and then at the dead man. "I'll thank you later."

There was no time for discussion. Preacher jammed the revolver into the front of his pants with a grunt and turned back toward Lieutenant Adams. He grabbed at the man as he slid halfway down the rockface. Preacher groaned under his breath as he pulled the man over his shoulder and felt his optimism drain away with his dwindling supply of energy. He was so tired. A verse from an old gospel hymn came to mind. *I'm going to lay down my burden, down by the riverside, down by the riverside.* Preacher grimaced at the irony of that song coming to him in his present circumstances. He wished the words were true. He began to hum the remembered phrase under his breath over and over between gasps. His body resisted the urge to look back and check on his companions. Twisting around took energy.

Guiding a blinded man took energy too. Bronco pulled Sarge forward while the man continued to blink his eyes while fanning the area rapidly with his free hand. Bronco stumbled across the body of the dead Rebel and turned to Sarge.

"Sergeant, you're going to grind that stuff in and blind yourself."

"I'm already blind," Sarge shouted back. "I just want to tear my eyes out!"

Bronco wondered if the grit could ever wash away. But that had to wait. He struggled ahead, praying that Sarge would keep his grip on his coattail. He remembered his grandmother's blindness, and it made him want to strike out angrily at the older man risking his sight behind him. He retrained himself and instead yelled encouragement.

The roar of Union artillery fire lobbing explosives announced their arrival and slowed the Rebels' advance, but it took the three men another twenty minutes to finally stumble into camp. Preacher almost went to his knees. But, instead, he steadied himself and lunged on for another hundred yards toward a tent marked with a cross.

Sarge flopped over on his back and pried his eyes open. He instructed Bronco to douse them with water from his canteens. At last, Bronco knelt over him and managed to flood the remaining grit from Sarge's eyes.

That accomplished, Bronco allowed himself to roll loose-jointed onto his back and imagine how blissful it would be never to get up.

Preacher didn't bother to look back at the men but pressed on alone until he could lay the lieutenant's limp body just inside the medical tent. He looked up forlornly at a medical orderly and crawled off a couple of yards to the side out of the way. The orderly knelt beside the officer and tried to detect signs of life. He stripped back the lieutenant's sodden coat. The metallic smell of the young man's blood mingled with the pungent odor of the medical supplies used to douse uncountable wounds. Preacher's assessment was dire, but he tried to hold on to a spark of hope.

The orderly held a small mirror under Lieutenant Adam's nostrils to detect any breathing. Preacher's panting subsided as he studied the young man's face, now peaceful and white in repose. He knew he would never forget from this moment the lank blond hair, the blind eyes, and the way the lips parted, revealing teeth only a little stained from tobacco.

"Is he going to make it?" It felt unbelievably daring to ask. The orderly looked over at the exhausted corporal and shook his head as he pulled the mirror away.

"Sorry, Corporal, he's gone."

Preacher struggled upright and looked down at his friend. He thought of Sarge's eyes and his own close call with the southerner's shotgun and smiled grimly at the notion that any of them expected to survive. Then Preacher reminded himself, as he so often did, that a higher power devised the steps they all took and the ways that they would all meet their ends. When he and the lieutenant first met, Adams had seemed hardly more than a teenager. Now, lying still and white, he seemed not to have aged at all.

As was his habit, Preacher prayed his thankfulness then for survival of the three remaining men. A few minutes passed before he stumbled out of the tent and gazed off across the camp.

Then he looked back toward the medical tent and found the form of his young friend who died for a worthy cause. He tried to balance that waste of life against the continuing lives of Sarge and Bronco, who, by some miracle, lay exhausted, only a hundred yards away. The infinite complexity of that equation overwhelmed him. He closed his eyes for a moment. There was honor here but no glory.

THE END

THE AUTHOR

Charles Reed is the author of the *Pursuers Series.- Trouble in Harlon County* (The first novel of The Pursuers Series), *Mission in Harlon County* (The second novel of The Pursuers Series), *Justice in Harlon County* (The third novel of the Pursuers Series), *and The Long Caper*, a time travel adventure to Harlon County.

Charles was born in Saint Louis, Missouri. Because of his father's occupation, he moved often throughout his early years. During that period, he attended twelve schools in four states. When not writing, Charles is an avid reader of biography, history, and historical fiction,

Charles has run three marathons, three half marathons, numerous *Tulsa Runs,* and ridden his bicycle in the Free-Wheel across Oklahoma six times. In addition, Charles has traveled in Europe, the Orient, and South America. His first trip by air was to Southeast Asia where he served in the infantry with the 101st Airborne Division. And finally, Charles is a "throw the seed down and see what happens" gardener.